"What man doesn't want a heart-shaped cookie cutter?"

"I'm sure this will *kumme* in handy when I host my annual Valentine's Day party," Turner joked.

"Your annual Valentine's Day party? Why haven't I ever been invited to that?" Tessa crossed her arms, pretending to feel slighted.

"Because this is the first year I'm having it," Turner replied without missing a beat.

Tessa giggled. "There's something else I have to confess about my discussion with Rhoda. Because I told her you'd given me a ride to the store, she made the assumption you were courting me."

"That's all?" Turner asked. "Why would that offend me?"

"Because I didn't deny it. I allowed her to think you wanted to keep our courtship a secret."

"As long as you're not upset about Rhoda making that assumption, then neither am I."

"I'm not upset," Tessa confirmed.

Why? Because it isn't true so it doesn't matter what Rhoda thinks, or because you'd accept me as a suitor? Turner wondered.

But even discussing a courtship between them caused warmth to course through every fiber of his being…

Carrie Lighte lives in Massachusetts, where her neighbors include several Mennonite farming families. She loves traveling and first learned about Amish culture when she visited Lancaster County, Pennsylvania, as a young girl. When she isn't writing or reading, she enjoys baking bread, playing word games and hiking, but her all-time favorite activity is bodyboarding with her loved ones when the surf's up at Coast Guard Beach on Cape Cod.

Books by Carrie Lighte

Love Inspired

Amish Country Courtships

Amish Triplets for Christmas
Anna's Forgotten Fiancé
An Amish Holiday Wedding
Minding the Amish Baby

Minding the Amish Baby

Carrie Lighte

HARLEQUIN® LOVE INSPIRED®

Recycling programs
for this product may
not exist in your area.

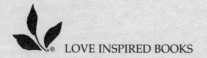

LOVE INSPIRED BOOKS

ISBN-13: 978-1-335-53892-5

Minding the Amish Baby

Copyright © 2018 by Carrie Lighte

All rights reserved. Except for use in any review, the reproduction
or utilization of this work in whole or in part in any form by any
electronic, mechanical or other means, now known or hereafter
invented, including xerography, photocopying and recording, or in
any information storage or retrieval system, is forbidden without
the written permission of the editorial office, Love Inspired Books,
195 Broadway, New York, NY 10007 U.S.A.

This is a work of fiction. Names, characters, places and incidents are
either the product of the author's imagination or are used fictitiously, and
any resemblance to actual persons, living or dead, business establishments,
events or locales is entirely coincidental.

This edition published by arrangement with Love Inspired Books.

® and TM are trademarks of Love Inspired Books, used under license.
Trademarks indicated with ® are registered in the United States Patent
and Trademark Office, the Canadian Intellectual Property Office and in
other countries.

www.Harlequin.com

Printed in U.S.A.

If we confess our sins,
he is faithful and just to forgive us our sins,
and to cleanse us from all unrighteousness.
—*1 John* 1:9

For everyone who loves and nurtures the children of others as if they were their own, and with special thanks to my brother.

Chapter One

"Soup from a can?" Tessa Fisher's mother, Waneta, asked incredulously. "None for me, *denki*. I'll just have bread and cheese."

If her mother turned her nose up at canned soup, Tessa figured she wasn't going to have an appetite for store-bought bread, either. She racked her brain for something else to offer her parents, who had arrived unexpectedly for Sunday dinner.

It was an off Sunday, meaning Amish families held worship services in their homes instead of gathering as a community for church. Tessa should have anticipated guests, since Sunday visiting was a cherished Amish tradition. But the truth was, as a woman living alone, Tessa was more likely to be the one dropping in on others than the one receiving visitors in the little *daadi haus* she rented from Turner King. Still, she hadn't imagined her parents would travel all the way from Shady Valley, which was two towns over, to Willow Creek, Pennsylvania. Since Tessa returned from worshipping at her sister's house only a few minutes before they arrived, she was caught unprepared.

"I'm sorry, *Mamm*," Tessa apologized as she set a bagged loaf on the table. "If I had known you were coming, I would have made something ahead of time, like a dessert."

"From a mix?" her mother half jested, untwisting the tie from the plastic bag.

When Tessa put her mind to it, she could bake and cook as well as any Amish woman, but those weren't her favorite responsibilities and she didn't see much point in laboring over large meals when she had only herself to feed. She'd much rather spend her time socializing or working extra shifts at Schrock's Shop, the store in town where she was employed as a clerk selling Amish-made goods primarily to *Englisch* tourists. Besides, it was the Sabbath. No one prepared a big dinner on the day of rest.

"Probably," Tessa admitted. "It's quicker that way."

"Since when is quicker better?" Waneta frowned. "It sounds as if the *Englisch* customers at Schrock's Shop are influencing our *dochder*, Henry. I think it's time she moved back home."

Tessa's father grunted noncommittally as he served himself several thick slices of bologna. At least the bologna was homemade, although not in Tessa's home; she purchased it the day before at Schlabach's meat market.

Tessa stifled a sigh. A little more than two years ago she and her sister, Katie, who were the youngest children and the only girls in their family, moved from Shady Valley so Katie could serve as a replacement for Willow Creek's schoolteacher, who resigned to start a family. Although Katie was twenty-three at the time, Henry and Waneta were reluctant to allow her to live alone, something Amish women in their area seldom did. So, they sent Tessa, who was nearing twenty-one, to live with her. Early last November, Katie married Mason Yoder, a farmer, and moved into a small house Mason built on the Yoder family's property. Ever since then Tessa's mother had been pressuring Tessa to return home, which Tessa was reluctant to do. Although she loved her parents deeply, Tessa sometimes felt stifled by their overly protective attitude, and she cherished her friends and job in Willow Creek too much to leave. Yet, she also knew the Lord ultimately required her to honor her parents, no matter how old she was or how much she disagreed with their opinion.

"The customers aren't influencing me, *Mamm*," Tessa protested. "Besides, I couldn't leave Joseph Schrock shorthanded at the shop, especially since I didn't have any experience when I first applied for a job there. You remember? He hired me with the agreement that if he took the time and effort to train me, I'd remain a loyal employee for as long as he needed me. I can't walk away now—you and *Daed* always taught us to abide by our commitments."

Tessa knew her mother wouldn't argue with her own instructive advice. As Henry silently chewed his bologna, Waneta slathered a slice of bread with butter and then held it up in front of her.

"The way to a man's heart is through his stomach," she said. "You'll never catch a husband with food like this."

To Tessa, it sounded as if her mother were discussing laying a trap for a wild animal. If she had known serving store-bought bread was going to result in a discussion about her likelihood of matrimony, she gladly would have baked a dozen fresh loaves to avoid the topic. Most of the area's Amish youth were discreet about if and who they were courting, and their parents seldom interfered in their children's romantic pursuits. But, at nearly twenty-three years old, Tessa knew her mother feared she'd never wed, and Waneta's strongly worded hints were gaining in frequency.

"I'm in no hurry to get married," Tessa replied. She'd had her share of suitors over the years, but in the end they didn't seem compatible enough for her to imagine devoting herself as a wife to any of them. Nor could she imagine taking on the duty of raising a family. Not yet, anyway. Not when she'd just begun to experience the rare opportunity of being a single Amish woman living entirely on her own, without the responsibility of cooking, cleaning or taking care of anyone else in her household. She added, "There aren't many eligible bachelors in Willow Creek, anyway."

"Which is exactly why you ought to *kumme* home. I've been talking to Bertha Umble and her *suh* Melvin isn't walking out with anyone."

Melvin Umble? It was hardly a wonder. The last time Tessa saw him when she was visiting home, Melvin seemed far more interested in sprucing up his courting buggy than he was in an actual courtship, and he'd spoken endlessly on the topic. Tessa let her mother's comment hang in the air.

"Would you like a cookie, *Daed*?" she asked. "They're packaged, but they're tasty."

"How can I refuse? Apparently, it's the way to my heart," her father replied with a grin, and Waneta playfully swatted at him with the back of her hand.

"Henry!" she exclaimed. "I'm only trying to help our *dochder*."

Deep down Tessa knew it was true that her mother *was* trying to help. But that was just it: Tessa didn't need help because she was perfectly content in her present circumstances. More than content, she was *happy*. As far as she was concerned, she could live as a single woman indefinitely.

"Please think about what I said," Waneta advised later as the three of them bundled into their woolen coats. They planned to spend the rest of the afternoon at Katie and Mason's house. No doubt Tessa's sister would serve a full supper in the evening. Although cooking a large meal wasn't permitted on the Sabbath, Katie's Saturday leftovers were bound to be savory and numerous.

"I *always* think about what you've said, *Mamm*," Tessa replied, hoping to reassure her mother that she needn't worry about her daughter living alone. "Nothing you and *Daed* taught me is ever far from my mind."

"Nor are you ever far from our hearts and prayers," Henry said.

"That's very true, but I still wish she weren't far from our *home*, either." Waneta couldn't seem to resist dropping one more hint as they stepped outside onto the small porch, but Tessa sensed it was far from her final one.

"Hallich Nei Yaahr," Turner King greeted Tessa and her parents as he approached the *daadi haus* on the front corner of his property.

Although January was soon over, because they hadn't seen him since the New Year began they wished him a happy new year, too. He extended a few colorful envelopes to Tessa. Since they technically lived at the same address, they shared a mailbox at the end of the lane. Usually, they gathered their own mail separately, leaving each other's items behind, but these messages appeared to be belated Christmas cards and there was wet weather on the way. Turner didn't want them to get ruined, so he delivered them on his walk back from the mailbox. "These were piling up," he said.

Tessa's mother clucked as her daughter accepted the mail. "She'd forget her own head sometimes," Waneta commented. "What if one of those had been an urgent message from home, Tessa? It's a *gut* thing we have Turner nearby to look after you."

Turner noticed Tessa's olive complexion breaking out in a rosy hue. As she stood next to her father, it was plain to see she'd inherited her prominent cheekbones and long, elegant nose from his side of the family. Turner bristled when his sister-in-law Rhoda once made the superficial remark that she wasn't sure if she thought Tessa was the most striking woman in Willow Creek or just plain homely.

But observing Tessa and her father now, Turner understood what Rhoda meant: one couldn't help but notice their unusual features, which differed drastically from those of most of the Amish *leit* in their district. For his part, Turner found their uniqueness becoming, and it was enhanced when father and daughter stood side by side. For a moment, he was distracted by how winsome she appeared. *I shouldn't be entertaining such a thought—Tessa's closer to my little sister's age than to mine.*

"*Denki* for bringing these to me," Tessa said sheepishly.

"It's not a problem. I forgot to collect my own mail until today, too."

"All the same, you will keep an eye on her, won't you?" Waneta persisted, as if talking about a *kind*. "Especially now that she's living alone, without Katie. We don't want her getting into any kind of trouble."

Tessa's dark, deep-set eyes flashed with apparent anger before she averted her gaze. Clearly, she was as uncomfortable with this conversation as Turner was. One of the reasons he didn't mind having renters was the Fisher girls mostly kept to themselves—at least, they did after he declined several of their invitations to supper when they first moved in. He valued his privacy and didn't relish the idea of increasing his interactions with Tessa beyond the brief greetings they exchanged whenever their paths crossed.

"Tessa knows where to find me if she needs assistance," he responded vaguely. Then he excused himself and hurried along the narrow lane leading up the hill to the larger house where he lived by himself.

As he walked, he marveled over the irony of Tessa's mother asking him to keep an eye out for her daughter. If only Waneta knew

Turner hadn't been able to keep his own sister, Jacqueline, away from a world of trouble, she wouldn't entrust Tessa to his watch.

Not that Tessa needed monitoring anyway. During the two years Tessa and Katie lived in his family's *daadi haus*, the sisters always paid their rent on time and they kept the house and yard tidy. Admittedly, they often had visitors, including church members, their parents and female friends for sister days. Turner noticed Mason Yoder used to frequent the *daadi haus*, too, but like any suitor who called on the Fisher girls, he only stayed long enough to pick Katie up and drop her off. Aside from when they hosted a few raucous volleyball games in their yard with other single youth from church, the sisters were courteous, sensible tenants.

Granted, Turner had conversed more often with Katie than with Tessa. The younger sister's effervescent personality frequently made him feel bumbling and dull by contrast. Rather than grow tongue-tied in Tessa's presence, he preferred to interact with Katie regarding any issues that had arisen with the *daadi haus*. Now he wondered if Waneta's comments indicated Tessa was a little too high-spirited for her own good. Maybe there was a reason unbeknownst to him behind the mother's request. He understood how family members sometimes protected each other's reputations; that's exactly what he was doing for Jacqueline.

"It was difficult enough raising my own siblings. I don't need to look after a fully grown tenant," Turner grumbled aloud as he entered his empty house.

He tossed a couple of logs into the wood stove and then washed his hands before preparing a plate of scrambled eggs for supper. He thanked the Lord for his food, adding, *Please keep Jacqueline safe from harm and bring her home soon.*

Before opening his eyes, Turner rubbed his thumb and forefinger back and forth across his brows. It seemed he'd had the same unrelenting tension headache for fourteen years. It started the day his parents were killed by an automobile when he was eighteen and he was left to raise Mark, Patrick and Jacqueline, who was a toddler at the time. If his aunt Louisa, then a young widow, hadn't been living in the *daadi haus* that once belonged to his grandparents, Turner never would have made it through those early years. She helped manage the children, especially Jacqueline, and he supported the family financially by taking over his father's buggy shop. But the year Jacqueline turned ten Louisa married a mason from out of state and moved to Ohio.

With the grace of God, Turner managed to raise his brothers according to their Amish faith and traditions. But bringing up a girl— especially one who was entering her teens— was a challenge exceeding Turner's best efforts. It wasn't that Jacqueline was necessarily unruly; it was more that Turner suddenly was at a loss for how to communicate effectively with her. Having completed her schooling at fourteen, she was no longer considered a child, but neither was she an adult. To Turner it seemed she wanted all the privileges of adulthood without any of the responsibilities, and the brother and sister frequently locked horns. When Jacqueline turned fifteen, she moved to Louisa's house in Ohio. By sixteen, her *rumspringa* began, and she suddenly left Louisa's to live among the *Englisch*. Much to Turner's consternation, it had been nearly eight or nine months since she'd contacted their family.

Raising his head, Turner released a heavy sigh. Try as he did to cast his burdens upon the Lord, lately he felt more overwhelmed than usual. He supposed this was because after his youngest brother, Patrick, married Rhoda and moved out of the house in November, Turner didn't have anyone to distract him from his thoughts on the weekends, when he tended to worry more about Jacqueline's welfare and sometimes took trips to search for her. It was on Saturday and Sunday evenings when he most wished for the loving support and companionship of a wife, but marriage wasn't an option that seemed probable for him.

As a younger man, Turner's time and energy were wholly consumed by raising and providing for his siblings. He'd expected he'd have more flexibility once they entered their teens, but in many ways Jacqueline's disappearance limited him more now than caring for her as a child had done. How could he court anyone when his weekends were spent searching for his sister? Furthermore, he couldn't imagine sharing the secret of Jacqueline's circumstances with anyone outside the family. Although Jacqueline hadn't been baptized yet so she wasn't in the *bann*—or shunned—it was still considered disgraceful for her to have run away to the *Englisch* world.

As for marrying in the future, Turner felt he couldn't risk starting a family of his own, for fear his wife would bear daughters. What if he failed to raise them to stay true to their

Amish faith and traditions as miserably as he'd apparently failed to raise his sister? He couldn't bear that kind of heartache again, nor could he allow his wife to suffer through it, either. No, despite his desire to marry, Turner figured the Lord must have willed for him to remain a lifelong bachelor.

Exhaling slowly, he reminded himself the next day was Monday and he'd be back in his shop with his brothers working at his side. Repairing and modifying buggies, crafting wheels and organizing inventory filled Turner with satisfaction. Unlike in the situation with his sister, there was almost no problem he couldn't figure out and fix in his workshop.

He lifted a forkful of eggs to his mouth, but they'd already gone cold. What he wouldn't do for a home-cooked meal—the kind his aunt used to make or his mother before that. He'd received many Sunday supper invitations, but for the past year he'd turned them down, anxious his hosts might question him about his sister. The last anyone in Willow Creek knew, Jacqueline was at Louisa's in Ohio, and he preferred to allow them to think that was still the case. After living among the *Englisch* for over a year, she'd have enough explaining to do and attitudes to overcome when—or *if*—she returned to their community. She didn't need rumors to begin before she'd even arrived.

Unfortunately, his isolation also meant Turner rarely enjoyed a hearty meal, unless one of his sisters-in-law made it for him. They didn't know about Jacqueline's disappearance, either, despite their expressed curiosity about her whereabouts. The three brothers rarely discussed Jacqueline's absence, even with each other, but Turner knew Mark and Patrick felt as concerned about their little sister as he did and they were equally committed to guarding her against gossip, even if their wives' questions—especially Rhoda's—were well intentioned.

As he prepared for bed that night, Turner again reflected on his brief encounter with Tessa's parents. If he'd been as protective as they were, might Jacqueline still be part of their family and community? Or had he been *too* strict? Was that what caused her to leave? There hadn't been any significant conflict between them when she'd gone to live with Louisa. In fact, all three of them had agreed it would be beneficial to have a female influence guiding Jacqueline as she entered womanhood. Turner certainly didn't blame Louisa for his sister's running away, but in retrospect, he regretted allowing Jacqueline to leave Willow Creek in the first place. What if by letting her go he'd given his sister the idea she wasn't dearly wanted, an integral member of their family? Turner shuddered. Once again, he asked the Lord to keep her safe and warm, to guard her against sinful temptation and to bring her home soon.

The pain that had been plaguing Turner all day moved from his forehead down the side of his jaw and into his neck. As his head sunk into the pillow, he decided no amount of distress was worth such physical discomfort. He had to stop worrying, keep praying and start working harder at finding his sister. Meanwhile, he wasn't going to be his tenant's keeper, no matter how insistent her mother was.

When the new day dawned, Tessa practically leaped out of bed. She loved Monday mornings, when she returned to her job at Schrock's. Initially, because her parents sheltered her so closely, she had little experience interacting with the *Englisch*, and she barely spoke a word to the tourists. But after two years as a clerk, she'd grown accustomed to the *Englischers*' ways and she readily struck up conversations as she assisted them with their purchases. Although she missed her close friend, Anna Chupp, who quit clerking when she got married, Tessa enjoyed engaging with the Schrock family and other Amish *leit* who consigned their goods in the shop.

"*Guder mariye*," she greeted Joseph when she entered through the back door.

"*Guder mariye*, Tessa," he said, pushing his glasses up the bridge of his nose. "Before you go into the gallery, I'd like to have a word with you."

"Of course. What can I do to help?"

Joseph smiled wanly. "Your willingness to be of assistance makes it very difficult for me to tell you this, Tessa. But you know our holiday sales weren't what I hoped they'd be this year. Now that *Grischtdaag* has passed and *Englisch* schools are back in session, there will be fewer tourists passing through Willow Creek until the weather warms. I'm afraid I temporarily have to reduce your hours."

Tessa's stomach dropped. "By how much?"

"I can only schedule you to clerk on Saturdays," Joseph confessed, shaking his head. "If I had my druthers, I'd keep you on full time and release one of the other employees, but of course I can't do that."

No, because that would mean releasing Melinda Schrock, the clerk who recently wed

Joseph's nephew, Jesse. Tessa understood family came first.

"I see," she said plaintively.

"It's only for a season. When spring rolls around, I'll have you back to full time again."

There was only one problem with Joseph's plan: without a steady income, Tessa wouldn't be able to pay her rent. She'd have to move back home before spring ever "rolled around." And once she did that, there'd be no escaping her mother's matchmaking attempts—not unless she got married, anyway.

Some escape that would be, she thought later as she fidgeted in bed long past midnight, mentally calculating her savings and racking her brain for another temporary employment opportunity, some job she could give up at a moment's notice in order to return to the shop. In the end, the only solution she could devise was asking Turner if she could postpone making her rent payments until her work schedule picked up again—something she was hesitant to do. Turner had already been more than generous in allowing her and her sister to live there, renting the *daadi haus* at a fraction of what he could have required. He even reduced Tessa's rent when Katie moved out. Although she'd be asking for only an extension, not a reduction, of her payments, she didn't want to take advantage of his benevolence. Nor did she want him to think she was irresponsible; her mother's recent comments to him on that subject had been humiliating enough.

More than that, Tessa was reluctant to speak with Turner because she harbored a sense of self-consciousness in his presence. When she and Katie moved in, Tessa had developed a full-fledged crush on Turner, who was sinewy and tall and whose tempestuous blue eyes and reticent nature gave him an air of mystery. That he'd been so well respected in the community and so charitable about their rent made her like him all the more. As a result, she tended to become highly animated whenever she spoke to him, sometimes making frivolous remarks because she was nervous in his presence. But he never accepted the sisters' invitations to share Sunday supper with them and their friends at the *daadi haus*, and Tessa suspected he was put off by her obvious interest in him. Eventually, she conceded Turner was too unsociable for her liking anyway and she gave up trying to get to know him better.

Indeed, over time she observed how often he wore a scowl across his face. While Turner wasn't quite ten years older than Tessa, she thought his countenance aged him. It apparently kept people at a distance, too, including his own sister. It was rumored Jacqueline had gone to live with her aunt the year Katie and Tessa moved into the *daadi haus*, and the girl hadn't paid her brother a visit since then. Tessa wasn't altogether surprised. Although Mark and Patrick King were generally congenial, she couldn't recall the last time she'd seen Turner smile. She imagined his somber demeanor would have felt oppressive to his teenage sister, especially since Jacqueline was said to be naturally humorous and outgoing.

In any case, unless the Lord directed her toward another solution, Tessa resigned herself to asking Turner for an extension on her rental payments. Scooting out of bed, she put a prayer *kapp* on over her loosely gathered hair and prayed a simple prayer: *Lord, I don't know what else to do and I really want to stay in Willow Creek. Please reveal Your will for me in this situation. Amen.*

While still on her knees she heard the sound of tires crunching up the snowy lane. Curious, she rose, wrapping a shawl around her shoulders as she made her way toward the kitchen, where she turned on the gas lamp. Meanwhile, a succession of honks came from outside. Tessa couldn't imagine who would be so rude, but when she opened the door, she spotted a car reversing its direction and heading back toward the main road. She figured it must have been desperate *Englischers* who were lost and needed help finding their way. But if that was the case, why had the driver honked as if deliberately trying to wake the household, and then left as soon as Tessa appeared, without waiting to receive directions first?

As she was about to close the door, something at her feet caught her eye. She peered through the near dark. It was a basket of laundry, of all things! Tessa was aware Turner paid an Amish widow, Barbara Verkler, to do his laundry for him, but she was perplexed by the absurd manner and timing of its delivery. She lifted the cumbersome basket, brought it indoors and was about to put out the lamp when something inside the basket moved beneath the light cloth draped across the top. A mouse? She didn't need another one of those getting indoors. Tessa wrinkled her nose and gingerly lifted the fabric.

There, bedded snugly on a pillow of clothing and diapers, was a chubby, pink-cheeked, toothless and smiling baby that appeared to be about three months old. The infant kicked her feet and waved her arms, as if to say "Surprise!" But Tessa was beyond surprised; she was so stunned she staggered backward. Was this a joke? The baby flailed her limbs harder now and her smile faded as she began to fuss. Tessa realized the child wanted to be held, and as she lifted the baby from the basket, an envelope slid from the blanket onto the floor.

Sensing it would provide information about whatever prank someone was playing on her—she didn't think it was a bit funny—Tessa bounced the baby in one arm and opened the envelope with her other hand. The note said:

Dear Turner,
I'm sorry to leave Mercy with you in this manner, but I know I can count on you to take good care of her for a few weeks until I've had time to decide what to do next. Please, I'm begging you, don't tell anyone about this—not even Mark or Patrick, if you can help it.
Your Lynne

Tessa couldn't believe what she was reading. This baby was intended for Turner's doorstep, not hers; the driver must have seen the address on the mailbox and assumed Turner lived in the *daadi haus*. So, who was Lynne?

Tessa always assumed there was more to her serious, enigmatic landlord than what met the surface, but she never imagined he was guarding a secret like this. Before she had an instant to contemplate what to do next, someone pounded on the door. Had the driver realized his mistake and returned for the child?

"Tessa!" Turner shouted urgently, as concerned for her safety as he was annoyed about the disruption to his sleep. "It's me, Turner. Are you all right?"

When the door opened, Tessa was pressing a finger to her lips. "Shh. You'll upset the *bobbel*," she chastised, gesturing with her chin toward the baby she cradled in her other arm, its face obscured by Tessa's posture.

Taken aback, Turner lowered his voice and uttered, "A *bobbel*? What—"

"*Kumme* inside," Tessa directed. "There's something you need to read."

In the kitchen Turner took the note Tessa thrust at him. He scanned the message and upon noting its signature, a surge of wooziness passed from his chest to his stomach and down to his knees. Lynne—the girlhood nickname he'd given Jacqueline. Feeling as if he was about to pass out, he plunked down in a chair and covered his face with his hands.

His first thought was, *I've heard from Jacqueline*. Denki, *Lord!* But it was immediately followed by a rush of anguish over the circumstances surrounding her communication. His mind was roiling with so many questions, concerns and fears, he felt as if the room was awhirl.

When the dizziness diminished, he opened his eyes. Noticing a torn envelope lay on the table in front of him, he bolted upright again. "Why did you open my note?" he asked.

"If I had known it was meant for you, I wouldn't have!" Tessa huffed, swaying from side to side as she spoke. Turner could now see the baby clearly; her eyelids were drooping and her long, wispy lashes feathered her bulbous cheeks. "But when someone leaves a *bobbel* on my doorstep in the middle of the night, I'll search for any clue I can find."

"Who? Who left the *bobbel* with you?" Turner figured it wasn't Jacqueline—she wouldn't have made the mistake of leaving the baby at the *daadi haus* instead of up the hill.

"I assume by the car the person or persons were *Englisch*, but I didn't see the driver or if there were any passengers," Tessa responded. "Don't you know who Lynne is?"

"Of course I do," he affirmed, without

answering what he assumed Tessa really wanted him to tell her: Who *was* Lynne? "I just wasn't sure who dropped the *bobbel* off."

"'Dropped the *bobbel* off' is putting it mildly. This *kind* was *abandoned*," Tessa emphasized. "What kind of person does something like that in the dead of winter? If you want, I can stay here with Mercy while you go to the phone shanty."

"The phone shanty?" Turner repeated numbly. "Why would I go there?"

"I assume you'll want to call someone… like Lynne? Or the *Englisch* authorities?"

"Neh!" Turner responded so forcefully the baby jerked in her state of near sleep. *"Neh,"* he repeated in a whisper.

"Why not?" Tessa pressed.

Turner stalled, studying the baby. Even in the dim light and with her eyes closed, she was clearly his sister's child. With her dark tuft of hair, roly-poly build and snub nose, she looked exactly like Jacqueline did as a baby. "You know we respect the law, but we don't involve the *Englisch* authorities in private matters like these," he said, referring to the general Amish practice of managing their own domestic affairs whenever possible. "Mercy was left in my care because her *mamm* had an emergency. If you hand her to me, I'll take her home now."

Tessa hesitated before placing the baby into Turner's arms. "Okay, but it will be easier for you to carry her in the basket. Let me fix this one so it's more comfortable and secure."

She left the room and when she returned, Tessa emptied the basket before placing a firm cushion on the bottom. Then she showed Turner how to swaddle the baby with a light blanket. She covered the lower half of Mercy's body with a quilt, emphasizing to Turner that it was only for the short walk to his house. "You probably already know this," she said, "but *bobblin* this age mustn't have any loose blankets in their cradles because blankets can cause overheating or even suffocation."

Turner shuddered to realize he *hadn't* known that. What other serious mistakes might he make?

Placing the contents of the basket in a separate bag, Tessa observed, "At least someone took care to pack *windle*, clothes, a bottle and some formula. Look, there are even instructions on how to prepare it and what time she eats."

"*Gut*, then I should be all set," Turner said, trying to project assurance.

Tessa arched an eyebrow at him. "Have you ever cared for a *bobbel* on your own before?"

"*Neh*, but I raised my sister from the time she was a toddler."

"That's not the same as caring for an infant this young."

Turner knew Tessa was right, but what else could he do? He felt duty bound to honor Jacqueline's request not to tell anyone about Mercy, so asking his sisters-in-law for help was out of the question. "That's my private matter to manage and I'd like it to stay that way," he said pointedly, turning toward the door.

"Wait," Tessa said. Surprised by the weight of her hand on his arm and the authority in her voice, Turner pivoted to look at her. The skin above the bridge of her nose was dented with deep lines, and worry narrowed her big brown eyes. "Mercy's sleeping now, but that won't last long. Joseph has temporarily reduced my hours at the shop, so I just work Saturdays now. If you'd like, I'm free to watch the baby during the day while you're at work."

Astonished by Tessa's willingness to help, Turner wondered if the solution could be that simple. From Tessa's brief interaction with Mercy, Turner could see how capable she was, but could he trust her to keep the situation a secret? Then he realized since Tessa already knew about the baby's arrival, he'd have to trust her to be discreet whether or not she cared for Mercy. It would be imprudent to refuse her offer.

"That would be *wunderbaar*," he admitted, "provided you don't tell anyone. I mean it, not a soul. I'll pay you, of course."

Tessa's eyelids suddenly snapped upward like a window shade as she took a step backward. "You needn't *bribe* me to keep this a secret, Turner!"

"*Neh*, I didn't mean I'd pay you for your discretion—I meant I'd pay you for your time."

Tessa softened her stance and reached to fiddle with Mercy's quilt. "That's not necessary. We're family in Christ, and you've been an excellent landlord to Katie and me. This is the least I can do in return. Besides, I want to help. Really."

Turner's ears warmed at her compliment. "And I very much *want* your help," he said. "But I insist on compensating you for it."

"Perhaps… Perhaps we could work out an arrangement with the rent? Since I won't be earning an income at Schrock's for several weeks—"

"I'll waive the next few months of rent entirely," Turner interrupted. "Now, I'd better get Mercy to the house before she wakes again."

"*Gut nacht*, Turner." Tessa held the door for him, adding, "Don't worry. It's only for a short time. Everything will be all right."

"*Jah*, I'm sure it will," he agreed. But as he trudged up the lane, he didn't feel at all confident about what the next few weeks would bring.

Chapter Two

Tessa lay in bed on her back with her eyes wide open. Who was Lynne? "Your Lynne" the woman had written. Usually that term was used to imply a close connection. Was Lynne a relative? A cousin, maybe? Since the Amish wrote letters in *Englisch* instead of in their spoken *Deitsch* dialect, Tessa couldn't discern from the note whether its author was Amish or not.

She shook her head, trying to stop the ideas that were filling her imagination, but it was no use. She remembered all the times she and Katie noticed Turner leaving on Saturday evenings, either by buggy or in a taxi. She knew it was wrong to speculate about his comings and goings and even worse to jump to unsavory conclusions about his actions and character. *Turner King is nothing if not upright*, she thought, forcing herself to consider the baby instead.

With her pudgy arms and cheeks and her pink skin, Mercy had obviously been well nurtured. At least, she was until her mother abandoned her. Tessa sighed. She supposed she couldn't really say the baby was *abandoned*. After all, it wasn't as if she'd been left with a complete stranger. Turner knew who the mother was, even if he wouldn't say. Tessa could only guess why the mother didn't speak to him directly about caring for the baby instead of just leaving Mercy on the doorstep. Maybe she truly was in a rush, but it seemed if she legitimately had an emergency, she would have called upon other relatives or friends who were better prepared to look after a baby than Turner was. And why did she insist on secrecy, even from Turner's brothers?

The entire situation didn't make any sense, but one thing was clear to Tessa: upon reading the note, Turner's expression changed from one of irritability at being woken late at night to a wide-eyed vulnerability that made him appear almost like a baby himself. Realizing stoic, self-sufficient Turner King was shaken and burdened filled Tessa with a sense of compassion and she was eager to help. Yes, she'd taken offense at his repeated admonishments not to tell anyone about the baby, but his distrust was a small affront compared with waiving her rent for the next few months as payment for caring for Mercy.

Granted, being a nanny wasn't her favorite job, but it was one she had a lot of experience doing. As a teenager the only way she could earn an income had been to mind children. In her community, when an Amish woman had a baby, the family often hired a girl like Tessa to watch the other offspring, so the mother could devote herself to the newborn. While Tessa had doted on the children under her care, she had wished there were other opportunities in Shady Valley for her to earn money. It was expected that most Amish women would marry and give up their jobs when they began families of their own. Even at a young age, Tessa realized she'd probably have her whole lifetime to keep house and care for children, so she'd wanted to experience a different kind of responsibility while she still could. That was why she was so attached to her job at Schrock's.

Yet right before she fell asleep, Tessa realized that although she wouldn't have chosen to be laid off from the shop any more than she'd wish an emergency on Mercy's mother, the timing was mutually beneficial for both her and Turner. It was so uncanny Tessa knew it had to be the Lord's answer to her prayers. He had delivered the alternate solution she'd just requested and she was grateful for it.

When she woke before daybreak, Tessa brewed a pot of coffee and then peeked out the back window of Katie's former bedroom. From this vantage point, she could see a light burning at the house on the hill. Were Turner and the baby awake already? Had they ever gone to sleep the night before? Figuring Turner wouldn't refuse a cup of coffee, she dressed, donned her winter cloak and bonnet, and trudged up the lane carrying the full pot. She heard Mercy's cries before she climbed the porch steps.

"Guder mariye," she said when Turner opened the door. He looked as if he'd spent the night chasing a runaway goat: his posture was crooked, his clothes were rumpled and his eyelids were sagging. "I know it's early but I thought you could use a cup of *kaffi*."

"I'm glad you're here." Motioning toward Mercy, he confessed, "I don't know what's wrong with her. I've fed her, burped her and changed her *windle*, but she keeps screaming."

"She probably misses her *mamm*," Tessa

said, setting the coffeepot on the table so she could receive the red-faced baby from Turner's arms. Rather, from his *arm*. Tessa noticed Mercy was dwarfed by Turner's size; he could have easily balanced her with just one hand. Yet he was every bit as gentle as he was adroit, and as he carefully passed the screeching baby to Tessa, she was aware of the way his arm softly brushed against hers.

While Turner filled two mismatched mugs with coffee, Tessa cooed, *"Guder mariye,* Mercy. What's all this fussing about, hmm? How can we make you more comfortable?"

Mercy's wailing continued as Tessa held the baby close to her chest. She asked Turner to place a quilt on the table and then she set the baby down and took notice of her clothes. Mercy's diaper was lopsided and gaping and her legs were cold and damp. "I think she needs a bath," Tessa suggested. "And I'll show you how to change her *windle* so they're secure."

"I didn't want to hurt her tummy by making it too tight," Turner said, amusing Tessa with his innocent but thoughtful mistake. This was a side of Turner she'd never seen before. "I'll go fill the tub."

"Neh, not the tub," she replied, chuckling blithely in spite of Mercy's screams. "She's

too small for that. We can bathe her in the sink. You get her ready, please, and I'll make sure the water is the right temperature."

Tessa rolled up her sleeves and set a towel in the bottom of the sink to serve as a cushion. Then she filled the sink part way and tested it with her elbow. She took Mercy from Turner and eased her into the water. Almost immediately Mercy stopped crying. Within seconds, she was smacking the water with her feet and hands, looking momentarily startled each time droplets splashed upward, but then she'd smile and slap the water again.

"She likes it!" Turner exclaimed.

Surprised by the brightness of his grin, Tessa threw back her head and laughed. "Most *bobblin* do, provided the water's not too hot and definitely not too cold," she said instructively.

After she washed, dressed and sufficiently fed Mercy using the supplies Lynne had provided, Tessa rocked the baby up and down in her arms. "She's getting drowsy," she observed. "You look exhausted, too. Why don't you go get a couple hours of sleep before you head to your shop? I'll stay here in the parlor with Mercy, in case she wakes up."

Turner twisted his mouth to the side and shook his head. "*Neh*, that's all right."

Tessa reflexively bristled; why was he so uneasy? It wasn't as if she was going to abscond with the baby to the *Englisch* authorities the first chance she got. "I'll take *gut* care of her and if anyone *kummes* to the house, I'll knock on your bedroom door right away," she assured him. "No one will ever know Mercy and I are here."

Turner rubbed his brow. Was he tired, apprehensive or in pain? It was difficult for Tessa to tell. Finally he said, "*Denki*, I'd appreciate that," and shuffled from the room.

"Now it's time for you to get some sleep, too, little *haws*." Tessa referred to Mercy as a bunny as she lowered the baby into the basket. "When you wake, we'll have a *wunderbaar* day, won't we?"

The comment was more of a wish than a promise. Tessa had spent enough time caring for little ones to know that sometimes it was an enjoyable, fulfilling experience, and sometimes it was tedious, demanding work. Tessa also knew there wouldn't be anyone else around for her to talk to. The very thought made her feel as if the walls were closing in. *It's only a short-term solution to ensure my long-term situation*, she reminded herself. *Besides, it's helpful to Turner and the Lord knows how much he needs that right now.*

Tessa tiptoed toward the kitchen to clean the sink and hang the damp towels, smiling about how loosely Turner had diapered Mercy and how delighted he'd been that she liked her bath. If grumpy Turner King could demonstrate good humor under his present circumstances, she could be cheerful, as well. Yes, she was determined to make today a wonderful day. For herself, for Mercy and for Turner.

Turner clicked the door shut behind him. While he was grateful for Tessa's suggestion to catch a nap before work, he had lingering qualms about her being in the house while he was asleep. Namely, he was nervous someone might stop by—not that that was likely to happen, since it rarely had before—and discover Tessa there, whether with or without the baby. While he knew there was no hint of impropriety in his or Tessa's behavior, he worried her presence there so early in the morning might tarnish their reputations.

But hadn't she promised she'd wake him instead of answering the door if anyone came by? Ultimately, he was too tired to worry an instant longer and he collapsed into bed. He was so exhausted from being up half the night with Mercy it seemed as if his head had just hit the pillow when Tessa rapped on the door.

"Turner, it's almost eight o'clock," she called. "Mercy's asleep in the parlor and I'll be in the kitchen."

As he opened the bedroom door a fragrant aroma filled his nostrils and Turner snuck past the dozing baby into the kitchen. "Something smells *appenditlich*," he said.

"I figured you'd need a decent meal to start your day. I made *pannekuche* and *wascht* but since there's no syrup, you'll have to use jam. It wasn't easy preparing something substantial. You must dislike cooking as much as I do—your cupboards are even emptier than mine."

Unlike most of the Amish *leit* in their district, Turner hadn't owned a milk cow, or even chickens, since Jacqueline left home. He relied on the local market for his dairy supply as well as for his other staples, and sometimes he neglected to shop until he was down to the last item in his pantry. He was surprised to hear Tessa's cupboards were often bare, too. Since she said she didn't like to cook, he was touched by her thoughtfulness in preparing their meal.

"Well, *denki* for making this," Turner said, sitting down at the opposite end of the table. It felt strangely intimate to eat breakfast alone with a woman. After saying grace, he told

Tessa, "Don't feel as if you need to cook for me in the future."

Tessa's gleaming eyes dimmed. What had he said wrong? He only meant he didn't expect her to do anything other than care for Mercy. If last night was any indication, she'd have her hands full enough as it was.

"Since Mercy was asleep, I didn't have anything else to do and I was getting hungry myself," Tessa replied, helping herself to a sausage.

Turner stacked pancakes on his plate and took a bite. They melted in his mouth. "Do you want to watch Mercy here or at the *daadi haus*?" he asked.

"Here, since I'm far more likely to get unexpected visitors at the *daadi haus* than you are."

Embarrassed Tessa noticed how seldom he received company, Turner swiped a napkin across his lips. "That probably would be best," he agreed.

Tessa continued, "Monday through Friday I can arrive as early as you like until Mercy's *mamm* returns. For the most part, I can stay as late as you need me to stay, too. But I do have occasional evening commitments I'd prefer not to miss."

Evening commitments. Did that mean she

was being courted? It was the customary practice for Amish youth in Willow Creek to court on Saturdays and to attend singings on Sunday evenings, not during the week. But for all Turner knew, it might be different for some couples, depending on how serious they were. He set his napkin beside his plate. "What time do you usually go out?" he asked.

Tessa's cheeks flushed and she swallowed a sip of water before speaking. "I didn't say I was going out."

Now Turner's face burned. He hadn't meant to be presumptuous. "Sorry. I assumed someone like you would be going out."

"Someone *like me*?" Tessa arched an eyebrow. "What am I like?"

Turner sensed he was wading into murky waters. "I only meant that you're young. You're social. You're, you know…carefree."

"Carefree?" Tessa echoed. "I'm not sure that's accurate. But, *jah*, sometimes I like to socialize on Saturday evenings. On Sundays after church, too, although I suppose I could change my plans if necessary."

So then, did that mean she was being courted or not? Turner didn't know why it bothered him that he couldn't be sure. "*Neh*, there's no need for that. I'll watch Mercy on the weekends—my brothers can tend shop on Saturdays, if needed."

Tessa dabbed the corners of her lips. Turner had never noticed how they formed a small bow above her slightly pointed chin. "On Wednesdays, Katie and I usually have supper together at the *daadi haus*. I suppose I could cancel, but I don't know what excuse I'd give her…"

"*Neh*, you shouldn't cancel," Turner insisted. "The last thing I want is for you to be tempted to create a false excuse. I'll be back in plenty of time for you to eat supper with your sister tomorrow evening."

He rose to don his woolen coat for the short stroll to the buggy shop on the western corner of his property. Setting his hat on his head, he hesitated when he heard Mercy stirring in the next room. His brothers were going to wonder what was keeping him and he didn't want them to come to the house, so he reached for the doorknob. Just then, Mercy began wailing in earnest and Tessa moved toward the parlor.

"Don't worry, I'm here," she said as she left the room.

Turner didn't know whether her words were intended for the baby or for him. As grateful as he was for Tessa's help, she also kept Turner on edge. *Is she a little touchy, or am I imagining it?* he wondered, hoping she wasn't temperamental enough to change her mind about protecting his secret or honoring their arrangement. But as he strode across the yard, he again reminded himself he had no choice but to trust her.

By noon, Turner and his brothers finished assembling an order of wheels for the Amish undercarriage assembler who owned a shop several miles away and partnered with the Kings. Although Mark offered to make the delivery, Turner insisted he'd do it himself. His reasons were twofold. First, he'd stop at an *Englisch* supermarket, where no one would look twice if he purchased formula for the baby along with food for himself.

Second, the trip would give him an opportunity to check out the area's minimarkets. According to Louisa, it was rumored among Jacqueline's acquaintances that Jacqueline had recently returned to the Lancaster County area, not far from Turner's home. Although his sister didn't have the required work permit, her peers said she supposedly was working in what the *Englisch* called a "convenience store." The term saddened Turner, especially when he saw what was sold at such shops. But he made a habit of stopping in at the area's stores under the pretext of buying a soda, hoping he'd bump into Jacqueline. He realized this method was about as precise as searching for a needle in a haystack with mittens on and his eyes closed, but it was better than nothing.

As usual, his Tuesday trip yielded no further clues about his sister's whereabouts and by the time he made his delivery, purchased groceries, returned home and stabled his horse, Turner's eyes were bleary with fatigue.

"Look who's here!" Tessa exclaimed when he walked into the parlor, and he grinned in spite of himself. Tessa was holding Mercy against her chest, one hand supporting the baby's legs in a sitting position, the other embracing her across her waist. As if in welcome, Mercy cooed and a long string of drool dangled from her lower lip.

"Let me get that," Turner said. As he gingerly removed the spit cloth from Tessa's shoulder to wipe the baby's mouth, his knuckles skimmed Tessa's cheek. "Sorry," he mumbled, his ears aflame, but she acted as if she hadn't noticed.

After Turner dabbed the baby's mouth dry, Tessa handed her to him. "I've made a list of items we'll need for the *bobbel*," she said.

A list? "I already bought formula when I was making a delivery."

"*Gut.* Did you pick up extra bottles, too?"

"*Neh*, I didn't think of that."

"It would be helpful to have another spare or two. Also, I'm concerned about Mercy sleeping in the basket. She can't roll over yet, but she's a good little kicker and I wouldn't want her to topple it."

"I might have a cradle stored in the attic. I'll look tonight."

"And then there's the matter of Mercy's *windle*. I'll use your wringer to wash them, but we ought to purchase cloth so I can cut a few more. I could do that in town but it might arouse suspicion."

"You're right," Turner replied, jiggling Mercy. "If you tell me what to get, I can pick the material up in Highland Springs the next time I make a delivery. But I don't have a wringer—I gave mine to Patrick and his wife when they married. Barbara Verkler does my wash for me. She picks it up from my porch on Monday morning and delivers it on Tuesday."

"Uh-oh. I knew about Barbara but I didn't realize that meant you didn't have a washer here at all. I'd better take Mercy's dirty *windle* home with me and wash them there."

"*Denki,*" Turner said, impressed Tessa thought of details about Mercy's care that never would have occurred to him. He followed her to the door and waited while she donned her cloak.

"I'll be glad to see you again tomorrow," she said, tapping the baby's nose.

Turner was surprised but pleased. "You, too," he replied, not realizing until too late that Tessa was speaking to Mercy instead of to him.

As soon as Tessa latched the door behind her the baby let loose a howl Turner couldn't quiet no matter how he tried. Tomorrow might as well have been a month away.

"Supper was scrumptious," Katie raved, cleaning her plate with a heel of bread. "Was the sauce actually homemade?"

"Jah," Tessa confirmed.

On Tuesday, although she'd enjoyed reading Scripture and praying quietly while Mercy slept, Tessa had begun to feel stir-crazy without having any tasks to do or anyone to talk to, so on Wednesday she had toted ingredients with her to Turner's house. Since she had time, she'd decided to forgo the jarred spaghetti sauce she usually bought and use fresh tomatoes and basil to create her own. Tessa had inwardly smirked when Turner gladly accepted the helping of meatballs and pasta she'd set aside, despite what he'd said about it being unnecessary to prepare meals for him.

After spending more time with him in the past few days than during the entirety of the time she'd lived in Willow Creek, Tessa expected to have gained better insight into his personality. Instead, she found him just as difficult to understand. Sometimes his response to her best intentions—such as when she'd prepared breakfast for him—bordered on disapproval. But at other times his appreciation for Tessa was obvious, such as when he'd clumsily indicated he couldn't wait to see her again or when he was retrieving a cradle for Mercy and he'd also brought a rocking chair down from the attic for Tessa to use.

"There's got to be another way you can earn enough money to pay your rent," Katie said, interrupting Tessa's thoughts. She spooned a generous helping of meatballs into a glass container. Both girls appreciated that Mason understood their need to spend time with each other, and they always made enough food for Katie to bring home to him. "I can speak with the *eldre* after school tomorrow. Maybe one of the families needs help around the house, or—"

"*Neh!*" Tessa vehemently objected. "*Denki*, but for now, I can make ends meet."

Katie cocked her head. "Are you certain?"

"Jah," Tessa replied, struggling to come up with an explanation that was both honest and convincing for why she didn't need a temporary job. "I have a little money in savings. Besides, I'm not certain when Joseph might need me back again, so I'd hate to commit to working for someone else and then have to quit as soon as I began."

"I suppose that's true," Katie agreed. "Are you going to tell *Mamm* and *Daed* you're not working at the shop?"

Tessa frowned. *"Neh,* not if I can help it. If *Mamm* finds out Joseph has no pressing need for me—even though it's only temporary— she'll say I'm no longer required to continue working for him and I should return home."

"Don't worry," Katie consoled her. "Unless she questions me directly, I won't say a word about it, but you know she has a knack for figuring these things out on her own."

"Jah, and if she does, I might as well pack my bags. There are only two things *Mamm* wants right now—for me to *kumme* home and for me to find a steady suitor and get married. The minute I return to Shady Valley, she's going to arrange for Melvin Umble to call on me. I just know it."

"That's the perfect solution!" Katie exclaimed, clapping. "We need to match you up with a suitor here."

"Oh, you mean so I don't get into an argument with *Mamm* about Melvin once I move back? I'm not sure a long-distance courtship would be enough to deter—"

In her enthusiasm, Katie cut Tessa short. "*Neh*, I'm not suggesting a long-distance courtship in the future. I'm suggesting a local one in the present. Think about it. If *Mamm* caught the slightest hint you already have a suitor here, she'd likely pay the rent for you to stay at the *daadi haus* herself!"

Tessa squinted suspiciously at her sister. Ever since Katie married Mason, she seemed eager to match Tessa up, too. Katie claimed it was because she valued finding a man she loved so much she wanted Tessa to experience something similar, but Tessa suspected Katie may have felt guilty about leaving her behind. There was no need; although initially Tessa was sorry to see her sister go, she quickly adjusted to living completely by herself and now she actually preferred it that way. Especially since Katie and Tessa still visited each other regularly.

"That may be true, but I've already been courted by the only eligible bachelors I can think of in Willow Creek," Tessa complained.

Everyone except Turner, that is, she mused, recalling how her skin had tingled when his hand accidentally touched her face the previous evening. She immediately banished the peculiar thought.

"In Willow Creek, *jah*," Katie said. "But Mason's sister-in-law Lovina has a brother who just moved nearby to Elmsville from Indiana, and he has expressed interest in remarrying."

"A widower? How old is he? Forty? Forty-five? Sixty?"

"Schnickelfritz!" Katie flicked a dish towel at her sister. "For your information, he's thirty-three."

"Is that how many *kinner* he has, too?"

"Of course not. David only has four *kinner*."

"Only?"

"Four isn't a lot. I hope to be blessed with at least that many." Katie brought the last of the dishes to the sink. "*Kinner* are a gift from the Lord, Tessa."

"I know that," Tessa replied. "But I can't imagine myself as a *mamm* to one *kind* yet, let alone four at once." As adorable as Mercy was, and as fond as she was becoming of the baby, Tessa had grown antsy after only two days of caring for her. She couldn't wait to get back to the shop where she'd be among people who could talk back to her when she spoke to them. "What do you think I have in common with this David, anyway?"

"I'm not sure," Katie admitted. "But you need a suitor and he wants a wife, so you ought to at least meet him. If you don't strike it off, that's fine, but you need to keep an open mind. You never know who the Lord might provide for you."

"How do you propose I meet him? It's not as if a thirty-three-year-old widower visiting from out of town is going to show up at one of our district's singings."

"That's why you're going to host a potluck supper here the next time he visits Willow Creek. Mason and I will *kumme*, and we'll invite Mason's sister, Faith, and her husband, Hunter. We can also ask Anna and Fletcher Chupp to *kumme*."

Tessa groaned. "But then it will be obvious you're trying to match David and me, which will be uncomfortable, especially if we have nothing in common."

"How about if Anna and Fletcher each invite a single friend, too?"

"I don't know…"

"Have you got any better ideas?"

"Neh."

"Then a Saturday evening potluck it is. I'll find out when David's going to be in town, and then we'll extend the invitations," Katie said, smiling.

Tessa wished she was as optimistic as her sister was, but she felt more dread than hope about meeting David. Still, it gave her the excuse to host a party and she supposed that if there was even the tiniest possibility Katie's plan would help prevent Tessa from returning home, it was worth a try. Somehow, though, when she weighed the option of becoming an instant mother to four children against the option of going home, going home didn't seem so bad after all.

Friday afternoon was especially challenging for Turner. For one thing, the shipment of LED components he'd ordered didn't arrive, which meant Patrick couldn't finish installing the new lighting system for Jacob Stolzfus's buggy. For another, Mark encountered a problem as he was working on the brakes of Jonas Plank's buggy. Unlike most of the buggies in Willow Creek, his used disc instead of drum brakes. Jonas said he kept going through brake pads too quickly, so Mark removed the calipers and when he saw how damaged the pads were, he examined the rotors, which were severely scored. The buggy would need new ones.

Because disc brakes were rarely used among the Amish, Turner had to call several *Englisch* salvage yards to find what he needed. Although it was permissible for the Amish in Willow Creek to use phones for business purposes, Turner didn't have one installed in the buggy shop, so he had to traipse to the phone shanty. It was quicker to walk than to hitch and unhitch his horse, but even so, the trip disrupted his regular work. He finally secured the parts from a place in Highland Springs, but the yard owner was going out of town and told Turner he couldn't pick them up until late the following Thursday afternoon. Jonas Plank pulled a face when Turner explained the situation to him, and it took all of Turner's self-control not to remind him he'd urged the young man to purchase a buggy with drum brakes from the start.

Then on Friday evening, despite Turner's best attempts to pacify her, Mercy cried so long and hard she eventually wore herself out. Between managing the challenges of his shop, taking care of the baby after work and struggling with his concerns about Jacqueline, Turner was bushed. After putting Mercy to bed, he stayed up just long enough to devour a ham sandwich before going to sleep himself.

Not long after, the blaring of a car horn jarred him from slumber. *Jacqueline's back!* he thought and bounded from bed to don his daytime clothes. His heart thumped as he shoved his feet into his boots, flung open the door and bolted outside onto the porch without a coat.

When the horn sounded again, he realized it was coming from the other end of the lane, near the *daadi haus*. A man's voice traveled distinctly across the winter air. "I'm not going to stop honking until you come out, Tessa!"

So it wasn't Jacqueline after all. Turner couldn't quite catch Tessa's reply to the man's demands, but her tone sounded alarmed so he hurried through the night in the direction of the ruckus. As he neared the *daadi haus*, he could hear Tessa scolding the driver. "I said hush! You're going to wake my landlord, who's a very grouchy person on a *gut* day, so I can't imagine how agitated he'll be if his rest is disturbed at nearly midnight by an *Englischer*. Please leave."

"It's not my fault I'm an *Englischer*," the man argued. "I'll become Amish if it means you'll go out with me. Just once. Please? I'll be a complete gentleman. We'll go out to eat, that's all. If you don't enjoy your time with me, I won't ask for another thing again. I promise."

"*Neh*, Jeremy. You need to leave. Now."

"Not unless you agree to go out with me."

"The only place I'm going is back inside, and I want you to leave."

The moon cast enough light for Turner to watch as Tessa started back up her walkway and onto the porch. Unsure whether he ought to interfere, he hesitated, but when the young man sounded his car horn again, Turner stepped out of the shadows. Suddenly all the frustration he felt about his sister living among the *Englisch* boiled up inside him and he struggled to suppress the urge to direct it toward the driver. The Amish were pacifists and Turner's faith required him to forgive both figurative and literal trespassers.

"Tessa asked you three times to leave. Do I have to ask you a fourth time?" he stated in a deep, gruff voice.

Jeremy's head swiveled in Turner's direction. "Of course not. I'm sorry for causing a commotion. I'll leave right away, sir," he said, his voice suddenly meek.

"*Denki*," Turner responded. "Please don't return without an invitation from me."

As Jeremy repositioned the car so he could

drive forward down the lane, the headlights circled the porch where Tessa stood clutching a shawl around her shoulders. Turner had never seen her dark, glossy hair loosened from its bun and he wasn't surprised Jeremy was smitten with her, considering the emphasis the *Englisch* placed on physical appearances. Still, Turner considered Jeremy's late-night visit an unacceptable intrusion and he wondered if this boisterous *Englischer* was the reason Waneta wanted him to keep an eye out for Tessa. Tessa had been baptized into the Amish church, so she wouldn't dream of becoming involved with an *Englischer* in any romantic capacity—about that, Turner had no doubts. But he worried she may be too guileless to realize her lively personality could be misinterpreted by young *Englisch* men who didn't understand her commitment to the Lord and the Amish way of life.

"I'm very sorry about that, Turner," she said. "Jeremy's parents own the *Englisch* diner on Main Street and he often stops by Schrock's, so I've chatted with him a few times. I'm surprised by his behavior tonight. Usually he's so well-mannered."

"As true as that may be, *Englischers* don't think the same way we do about, er, romantic relationships and courting, so you probably shouldn't give your address to them."

"I didn't give my address to Jeremy!" she protested. "His sister has given me a ride home before so she might have told him where I live, but I certainly didn't invite him here! I'd never do such a thing!"

Her adamant objection made it clear to Turner he was mistaken to think she would have been so naïve. Wanting her to know he'd stand behind her if Jeremy showed up again, Turner said, "That's *gut*. But he'll have to answer to me if he *kummes* here again without an invitation."

"He won't," Tessa firmly assured him, her chin in the air.

Turner got the sense she was offended, but once again he didn't know why. After saying good-night, he tromped back to the house. To his relief, Mercy was still sleeping soundly, which was exactly what he wanted to do. But when he got into bed, sleep escaped him. All he could think about was whether Jacqueline had been drawn into the *Englisch* world by a boy who promised he wanted only a single date and if she didn't like him, he'd never ask for another thing.

Then Turner questioned if he really came across as disagreeable as Tessa suggested. She had a lot of nerve, didn't she? Perhaps if she bore even a fraction of the kind of concerns and responsibilities he had, she wouldn't be so quick to judge. Or maybe if Turner were a younger man with little to worry about except which Willow Creek *maedel* he should court, he'd walk around wearing a ridiculous grin on his face.

Ah well, there was no sense dwelling on how his life might have turned out if he hadn't had to raise his siblings. He pulled the quilt to his chin and shut his eyes so he wouldn't be "a very grouchy person" come morning.

Chapter Three

Tessa was glad to be working at Schrock's Shop on Saturday instead of caring for Mercy, because she was peeved at Turner for assuming she'd told Jeremy where she lived. As if she would ever—quite literally—flirt with the *Englisch* world! Turner was worse than her parents, to suspect her of such a thing.

How hypocritical could he be, anyway? *He* was the one who'd had a baby delivered to his house by an *Englischer*, yet from the very start, she'd put every presumptuous, judgmental or otherwise nosy speculation out of her mind. She hadn't breathed a single meddlesome word to Turner about Mercy's mother and his relationship with her. But did he extend the same courtesy to her about her "relationship" with Jeremy? No. He'd made a snap judgment based on superficial circumstances.

Yes, it was better she put a little distance between her and Turner, lest she give him a piece of her mind.

Besides, after two additional days of speaking to no one except Mercy, Tessa was relieved to be back in the shop among other adults again. Entering the gallery, she inhaled the scent of homemade candles, soaps and dried-flower wreaths. The large shop also showcased furniture, toys, quilts and other specialty items made by the Amish *leit* in Willow Creek. She relished the experience of helping tourists select their purchases. Although a few customers over the years had been impatient or even rude when speaking with her, the vast majority were respectful. If they asked questions about her Amish lifestyle that she considered too intrusive, she was skilled at refocusing the discussion to the products at hand.

The shop's reputation for delivering high-quality goods attracted local *Englisch* customers as well as tourists, some of whom she knew by sight and vice versa, and they were always pleased to chat with each other. Tessa couldn't imagine ever enjoying a job as much as she enjoyed working in the shop.

Saturday morning was especially busy and she relished being in the midst of the hubbub.

During a momentary lull in ringing up sales, Joseph mentioned, "If business keeps up like this, I'll need you back full time sooner than I anticipated."

Tessa smiled at Joseph as she handed him a roll of receipt tape, but her mind was racing. What would she do about her commitment to care for Mercy if business soared and Joseph really did need her back sooner than expected? If he asked her to clerk more hours, she couldn't turn him down, not without offering a good reason. Obviously, she'd never tell Joseph about caring for the baby, but what would Turner do without her help? As galled as she'd been by his comments the previous night, she didn't have any intention of leaving him to manage Mercy on his own—for Mercy's sake, as much as for his. Tessa recognized she was probably being sentimental, but it didn't seem fair to break her budding connection with the baby, especially since Mercy had been left by her own mother once already.

For the rest of the morning she fretted about Joseph's offhand remark becoming a reality. It would be wrong to wish sales wouldn't increase at the shop, but she couldn't think of how else she'd avoid returning to work full time. Finally, after being so distracted she rang up a purchase incorrectly three times,

Tessa reminded herself the Lord knew all of their needs—hers, Joseph's, Mercy's and Turner's—and He would provide for those needs according to His sovereign providence and grace. During her lunch break, she retreated to a quiet area in the back room to pray, which alleviated her anxiety.

Her lunch consisted of an apple and a piece of bread thinly smeared with peanut butter, which she swallowed quickly, hoping to use the rest of her break time to purchase groceries at the market a few doors down on Main Street, since she hadn't had an opportunity to shop during the week. But as she headed through the gallery to the main exit, she noted a distraught young *Englisch* woman carrying a crying baby against her shoulder as she perused the merchandise in the soaps-and-salves aisle. Tessa recognized the woman from her previous visits.

"Shh, shh," the woman pleaded as the baby's volume increased. "Mommy only needs a few minutes and then we can go."

"Hi there, Aiden," Tessa addressed the baby, causing the woman to spin to face her. Tessa greeted her. "Hello, Gabby. Is there something I can help you find?"

"Hi, Tessa! I'm looking for goat's milk soap—the scentless kind. My husband has allergies so he can't use anything else, and Schrock's is the only place that carries it."

"It's on the middle shelf. Here," Tessa replied, reaching for a bar of the soap, which was closer to the size of a brick. "Is there anything else you're looking for?"

Gabby shifted the wriggling baby from one arm to the other as his screeching escalated. "I made a list of essential items I couldn't forget. I only have use of the car to get to Willow Creek once a month, but I don't think Aiden's going to let me finish my shopping today."

"Would you like me to hold him while you get what you need? I'm still on my lunch break."

The woman looked a little taken aback and Tessa didn't blame her. It was a forward thing to offer, but she'd grown so accustomed to calming Mercy when the baby was upset that she didn't think twice about volunteering to hold Gabby's baby.

"Or I could take your list and collect your items for you," Tessa suggested.

"Actually, *would* you mind holding him?" Gabby asked imploringly. "I'd be able to think a lot more clearly without him crying in my ear."

"Of course," Tessa agreed. "Take your time

and *kumme* find us when you're done. We'll be ambling around in the back."

"I'll just follow the racket," Gabby replied with a weak smile.

As Tessa strolled through the end aisle, she tried to soothe Aiden by rocking him every which way, but he was inconsolable. Mercy usually writhed like that when she had gas and Tessa suspected that was what was bothering Aiden, too. She lifted him to her shoulder and patiently tapped his back until he released a tremendous burp.

"Wow!" Gabby exclaimed as she rounded the corner with a canvas bag full of her purchases. "And I thought his *crying* was loud!"

"He feels better now, don't you, Aiden?" Tessa asked as she turned the infant so they could see his face. He glowered at them as if to ask what they thought was so interesting and then he lowered his eyelids, contented.

"Thank you so much," Gabby raved when Tessa passed the baby to her. "As much as I love him, it's a rare treat to do an errand without toting this fifteen-pound sack of bawling babyhood in my arms."

"You're *wilkom*," Tessa said. She certainly understood why Gabby was so frazzled. Tessa would be, too, if she rarely got out of the house without taking an infant along. Yet at the same time, holding Aiden made her feel a strange loneliness for the heft of pudgy little Mercy in her arms. Regardless of her indignation at Turner's comments the previous evening, Tessa decided after work she'd stop in at his house to see how he and the baby were faring.

Customers lingered in the shop until after closing time and because he needed the business, Joseph didn't hurry them away. By the time the doors were locked, the shelves restocked and the floor swept at Schrock's, the market down Main Street was closed. Tessa's grocery supply at home was limited to a few boxes of pasta, which she supposed she'd have to eat with butter and salt. So, when Melinda Schrock invited Tessa to join her and her husband, Jesse, and several others at the bowling alley, Tessa was tempted.

"Please?" Melinda cajoled. "We only have five people so far, which means we can't pair up for teams."

"I don't know," Tessa stalled. Usually, Tessa would have been the one who suggested the outing, but tonight she felt torn between joining her peers and getting back to see how Mercy was doing.

"It won't be a late night and we'll give you a lift home," Melinda persisted.

Tessa's stomach growled. The bowling alley, a popular location for the Amish in Willow Creek, made fantastic onion rings. Her mouth watering, she agreed, "Okay, if you're sure it's not going to be a late night."

But as it turned out, the only other person to join the trio at the lanes was Aaron Chupp, Anna's husband's cousin, which meant Tessa had to be his bowling partner. She suspected that Melinda, who once was courted by Aaron herself, was playing matchmaker on his behalf. Melinda could have saved herself the trouble. Tessa found Aaron to be unusually self-centered, a perception that was enhanced when he insisted they play several more frames—and then several more after that—when she expressed she wanted to head home.

Finally, they returned their bowling shoes and Melinda yawned exaggeratedly. "I'm so sleepy. Aaron, would you take Tessa home so Jesse and I don't have to go out of our way?"

"I'd be happy to," Aaron agreed, to Tessa's dismay.

All the way home, he spoke about himself and his work as a carpenter, never once asking her a question or pausing to allow her to interject a comment. Tessa found his monologue to be even less engaging than Melvin

Umble's discourse about his courting buggy, and she couldn't get inside her house soon enough. It was past twelve thirty, so when she peered through the window in Katie's room she wasn't surprised Turner's house was completely dark. He and Mercy were probably sound asleep, like Tessa should have been by now. As she pulled the shade she grumbled, "Some early night! That's what I get for falling for Melinda's tricks—and the onion rings weren't even that *gut*."

As she was brushing her hair, Tessa decided perhaps she'd drop in on Turner before she left for church the next morning. On Friday he'd indicated he wouldn't be going to worship services himself, but when she asked him how he'd explain his absence, he said that was his problem to address. She hadn't brought up the topic again, but maybe by now he'd changed his plans or his mind. It was possible he needed Tessa's help or input after all. *There's no harm in asking*, she thought as she extinguished her lamp and snuggled into bed.

Turner had been leaning against his porch railing when he heard the buggy coming up the lane some time after midnight. Aware that Tessa and Katie's horse died of old age the previous October, he deduced someone was bringing Tessa home. She'd probably made the most of her Saturday away from him and the baby, staying out as late as she pleased with her friends or possibly with her suitor. He didn't fault her for that. He'd found out early that day just how challenging caring for a baby could be—especially if the baby wouldn't stop whining. It took Turner nearly two hours of trying to pacify Mercy before he realized, upon changing her diaper, that she must have had a tummy ache. No sooner had he given her a bath, dressed her and swaddled her in a blanket than she'd soiled her new diaper, too. Dealing with Mercy's indigestion, the mess and his own frustration with himself at not being better at caring for her, Turner was worn out before the day hardly began.

Yet it wasn't Mercy's intestinal distress that kept him up past midnight; it was his own. His malaise began shortly after lunchtime with what he thought was his usual tension headache. Initially, he dismissed the accompanying upset stomach as a case of nerves because he was so anxious about not being present for the next morning's worship services.

Attendance at the twice-monthly church gatherings was of utmost importance in the

Amish community, and he'd never missed a service in his adult life. He agonized over his conflicting commitment to guarding Jacqueline's privacy and to the commandment not to forsake gathering together on the Sabbath. Obviously he couldn't show up at church with Mercy, nor could he leave her alone at home. He considered consulting his brothers, but then he'd not only violate Jacqueline's request, but he might put them in an uncomfortable position, too. Wouldn't they feel torn about keeping the secret from their wives?

The only person he could have brainstormed candidly with was Tessa, but when she broached the subject on Friday morning, he told her he'd work out the details himself. He had to admit the young woman had been extremely respectful about his privacy, never once nudging Turner for more information about the baby's mother or Turner's relationship with her. Over the past week, he'd begun to trust that she wouldn't deliberately betray his confidence. But he still figured the less Tessa knew, the less likely she was to accidentally let something slip. Furthermore, their church family was very close-knit and caring, but some of the *leit*—including his sister-in-law Rhoda—had a habit of asking nosy questions. Turner didn't want Tessa to be tempted to give a deceptive response to their queries.

After growing increasingly nauseated throughout the afternoon, Turner realized he wasn't merely plagued by anxiety: there was a physical cause for his symptoms. After several bouts of retching in the early evening he hoped to experience some relief, but instead his insides cramped tighter, and his torso and head became drenched with sweat. It was all he could do to feed and change Mercy and then put her to bed. He thought the night air might alleviate his nausea, so he wobbled onto the porch where he stayed until Tessa returned. After noticing the lamp go out at the *daadi haus*, he went back inside.

He had almost dropped off to sleep when his insides turned over and he had to bolt to the washroom. This pattern kept up for what felt like an unbearable amount of time. Just as his stomach finally settled down around four o'clock in the morning, Mercy woke up. Turner used his last spurt of energy to change and feed her, but when he returned her to the cradle, she let out an earsplitting objection until he gathered her again. Afraid he'd topple forward, he leaned against the wall, using his arms like a hammock to gently sway her back and forth until her eyes eventually closed. But as soon as he set her down, she kicked and caterwauled.

Turner was too feeble to do anything other than carry her to his bed with him. By the time he'd arranged her safely in his arm, he didn't have enough stamina to turn down the lamp. It didn't matter; he could have fallen asleep with his eyes open.

"Please, *Gott,* heal me soon and keep Mercy from illness," he mumbled, and the baby winced as his sour breath passed over her face.

This time his sleep was disrupted by a dream of Tessa standing on her porch, her long hair billowing behind her like a curtain in a breeze. "But it's not my fault I'm so grouchy," Turner was saying to her, in much the same way Jeremy had argued it wasn't his fault he was an *Englischer.* "I'll be a happier person if it means you'll let me court you. Just once. Please? After that, I'll never ask you for another favor again, I promise."

Turner woke with a jolt. In his delirium, he couldn't remember whether he'd really asked to court Tessa or if he'd dreamed it. *Either way, she probably said no—I'm not lively enough for her.* He groaned, and sleep overtook him again.

* * *

Having forgotten to set her battery-operated alarm clock, Tessa scrambled to get ready for church. Her intention to visit Turner before she left evaporated as she tied her dark winter bonnet over her good church prayer *kapp*. Services were being held at Rachel and Benjamin Coblentz's home, about two miles away. The roads were slick with ice and she'd have to walk quickly to make it in time.

The Coblentzes, like many other Amish families, used their basement for a gathering room, with the men sitting on one side and the women and small children in another area. Tessa was one of the last women to enter the room, sliding into a space on a bench near Melinda.

"Usually *I'm* the last in line," Melinda whispered. "You must have overslept. Does that mean you and Aaron went somewhere else after the bowling alley last night?"

Staring straight ahead, Tessa shook her head dismissively.

"Ah well, if you're fortunate, pretty soon the two of you will be courting, and you know how quickly courtship leads to marriage. Maybe by next fall you won't have to live all by yourself any longer," Melinda propounded.

Now Tessa was positive Melinda had been

playing matchmaker the evening before. Why didn't anyone believe she was genuinely content with her life as it was? Surveying the rows of benches in front of her, she supposed it was probably because most Amish women wouldn't voluntarily choose to live alone. Even the widows remarried quickly or else lived in relatives' homes or in *daadi hauses* on their relatives' properties.

The only other young Willow Creek woman Tessa knew who had ever chosen to live alone was Faith Schwartz, who had lived in an apartment above the bakery she owned. But that was only for a year—at Christmastime, Faith married Hunter, after Katie married Faith's brother, Mason, in early November. Melinda and Jesse were married during last autumn's wedding season, too. Tessa couldn't have been more pleased for her sister and friends, but she had other plans for herself, God willing. Why couldn't people accept that although she lived alone, she wasn't necessarily *lonely*? How could she be, with such a close family and community and relationship with the Lord? She honestly didn't feel like she was missing out on a thing. *Quite the contrary*, she thought for the hundredth time. *I like my life as it is.*

Asking the Lord to quiet her heart, she set

aside her ruminations to join in singing the opening hymns and concentrate on the minister's preaching. After the three-hour service, which was conducted in German, Tessa bustled upstairs with the other women to begin preparations for serving dinner. The men flipped and stacked the benches, transforming them into tables where the *leit* could stand as they lunched on cold cuts, cheese, peanut butter sweetened with molasses, bread, pickles, beets and an assortment of light desserts.

Tessa enjoyed chatting with the other women until it was her turn to eat, when she ravenously devoured generous helpings of everything except the beets. Homemade pretzels were also served that afternoon and she ate two of those, as well. Afterward she helped clear the tables and when Faith carried a tray of leftover cream-filled doughnuts into the kitchen, Tessa snatched one from the platter.

"These are so *gut!*" she exclaimed about the delectable treat from Faith's bakery.

"Denki," Faith replied. "I can wrap a few for you to take home if you like."

"That would be *wunderbaar,*" Tessa said, munching away. She didn't have any sweets, packaged or otherwise, in her cupboards. Faith wrapped two of the pastries in plastic and then left to help sweep the basement floor after the men loaded the benches into the bench wagon.

Tessa was setting her doughnuts on the side countertop so she wouldn't forget them when Katie emerged from the pantry. "Please don't tell me that's your supper," Katie chided over her sister's shoulder as she gave her a hug. Without pausing to hear Tessa's answer, she continued, "Speaking of supper, how about if we ask Anna and Faith to join us for our Wednesday evening meal? We can discuss our plan for getting together with you-know-who." Clearly, Katie was referencing David.

"You-know-who *who*?" Turner's sister-in-law Rhoda King inquired from where she suddenly appeared in the doorway.

Tessa shot Katie a look before replying evasively, "Oh, no one you know."

"Aha. I get it. It's a secret," Rhoda teased. "You're good at keeping secrets, aren't you, Tessa?"

Tessa's heart thudded. "What are you talking about?"

"A little birdie told us about your late-night surprise visitor last week."

How did Rhoda know about Mercy? Tessa removed a broom from its hook on the wall.

She needed to hold something to keep her hands from shaking.

"What late-night guest, Tessa?" Katie asked.

Tessa rolled her eyes and shrugged, as if she had no idea. She wasn't about to lie, but neither was she going to divulge Turner's secret. If everyone at church found out about Mercy, it wouldn't be from her.

"Jeremy Brown showed up at the *daadi haus* in the middle of the night!"

A surge of relief washed over Tessa—*Jeremy* was the late-night visitor Rhoda meant, not Mercy. Tessa bent to sweep crumbs into the dustpan as Katie exclaimed, "*Neh*, he didn't! What did he want?"

"Oh, you know how friendly Jeremy is," Tessa said. Most people in Willow Creek, *Englischers* and Amish both, were familiar with the Browns' diner on Main Street. The family was well liked and hardworking and Tessa frequently told Katie about her chats with Jeremy. "Sometimes he might be a little *too* friendly, perhaps, but he's harmless. On the contrary, he can be very helpful and he's demonstrated *Gott*'s love to his neighbors on Main Street on numerous occa—"

Rhoda interrupted, announcing, "He wanted Tessa to go out with him. Can you imagine? An *Englischer* showing up in the middle of the night to ask to date a baptized Amish woman?"

Katie looked concerned but she defended her sister by saying, "You seem to know a lot about the situation, Rhoda. Were you there, too, or was this information conveyed via the phone shanty?"

Rhoda completely missed Katie's implication her chitchat wasn't appreciated. "Neither," she answered candidly. "Melinda told me after Donna, Jeremy's sister, told her on Saturday afternoon when Melinda and Jesse ate lunch at the diner. Supposedly, afterward Jeremy was utterly mortified by his lapse in judgment, which might have had something to do with Turner threatening him off the property."

The notion that Turner would *threaten* anyone was absurd. "Turner asked him to leave, that's all," Tessa clarified, emptying the dustpan's contents with a loud tap against the side of the trash barrel.

"Maybe, but you know how menacing Turner looks. One glance at him and Jeremy probably lost sight of the fact the Amish aren't combative like *Englischers* are."

Despite her previous annoyance at Turner and her similar perception of his visage, Tessa reacted defensively to Rhoda's words before she had time to weigh her own. "I don't think Turner is menacing-looking at all. He has thoughtful eyes and a radiant smile!"

"Turner?" Rhoda made a choking noise. "Don't misunderstand. I have deep affection for my brother-in-law, but he's one of the glummest-looking people I've ever seen. Not that I blame him. He had to raise his siblings from a young age, and I suspect he had some trouble with his sister, since she never visits. I've tried to find out more about her, but he's pretty tight-lipped about her circumstances. Patrick is, too."

Remembering what the Bible said about a soft answer turning away wrath, Tessa bit her tongue before quietly suggesting, "Maybe they don't want their sister to be the object of the rumor mill, which can be very hurtful."

Rhoda jabbered on obliviously. "*Jah*, I suppose that could be the reason, but I sense they're hiding something. Of course, I'm only curious because I'd like to help Jacqueline if I could. I don't imagine it was easy growing up without her parents, especially her *mamm*." When her comment was met with silence, she continued, "Anyway, speaking of helping, we noticed Turner isn't in church today. He's never missed a gathering, so he must be awfully ill. We're going to stop at the house to see if there's anything we can do for him. Would you like a ride, Tessa?"

Tessa felt as if her limbs had turned to concrete. Rhoda and Patrick were going directly to Turner's house? She had to get there first. She couldn't let Rhoda discover the baby, not after she'd just released a string of gossip a mile long without so much as taking a breath.

"*Denki*, but I think I'll walk. I feel…lightheaded."

"You do look a little pale," Katie said as she turned from stacking plates in the cupboard. "How about if Mason and I stop by later with some *real* food for you for supper?"

"*Neh!*" Tessa responded. "I mean, the fresh air will do me *gut* and I'll probably take a nap this afternoon." It was no lie; she was suddenly exhausted.

"All right. Well, feel better then," Katie said, touching her sister's arm.

"I will." Tessa forced a smile as she lifted her cloak and bonnet from a peg on the wall. "See you Wednesday evening."

"And Anna and Faith, too, *jah*?"

"*Jah,*" Tessa agreed as she raced out the door in order to reach Turner's house before Rhoda did.

The thin layer of ice on the snow made tromping through the fields and up the hills to Turner's property a treacherous endeavor, but Tessa knew she'd never make it there in time unless she made use of the countryside's off-street shortcuts. She was halfway up the final hill when she lost her footing, landing hard on her knees and hands. Her skin stung where the icy crust tore her stockings and cut into her knees and wrists, but she picked herself up and charged forward. Her breathing was so labored from exerting herself in the cold weather that by the time she pounded on Turner's door, she felt as if her lungs would burst. Then she saw his disheveled, sickly appearance and it nearly took the last puff of her breath away.

Turner was as surprised to see Tessa on his porch as she apparently was by his appearance. Expecting at least one of his brothers and sisters-in-law would come to find out why he wasn't in church, Turner had been bracing himself for their arrival. As valiantly as he'd tried to protect Jacqueline's secret, he'd resigned himself to the fact he couldn't. The inability to honor her request now underscored his sense of having somehow failed her when she was younger. Despite his best efforts, he just couldn't seem to do right by her. The disappointment he felt in himself was even more enfeebling than his illness, and he propped himself against the doorframe for support.

"Turner!" Tessa gasped. "What's wrong with you?"

"The flu" was all he could say. He needed to sit. He wobbled into the parlor and sunk into the sofa.

Following him, Tessa asked, "Where's Mercy?"

From her room, Mercy began to cry, answering for herself. Tessa charged past Turner and up the stairs, returning moments later with the baby, who was dry and clean but restless from being in her cradle for a long stretch. Turner couldn't help it: he'd feared his arms would go limp and he'd drop her if he'd tried to lift her again.

"I expected Mark or Patrick," Turner mumbled as Tessa rocked Mercy, who stopped whining almost instantly. He noticed it wasn't the first time Tessa's actions were having a mesmerizing effect on both the baby and on him.

"They're on their way here any minute. That's why I came—to bring Mercy to my house before they got here."

He appreciated the gesture, but it was too late. "*Denki*, but they're going to ask why I wasn't at church today and I can't lie." His teeth knocked together as a chill rattled his body.

"Oh, look at you. You're shaking!" Tessa leaned over him to feel his forehead with her free hand. Her fingers were as cool and smooth as butter and he wished she'd let them linger there. Covering him with a quilt, she said, "You wouldn't have been able to go to church today whether or not Mercy was here. You're sick. That's the truth and it's all you have to say."

"I suppose you're right," Turner conceded after considering her suggestion. He added wryly, "I guess I should be thankful I'm so sick. Maybe it's a blessing from the Lord?"

But Tessa didn't seem to hear him. She set Mercy on a blanket near the wood stove. Almost as soon as she let go of the baby girl, the child started wailing, but Tessa was undeterred.

"I need to dash if I'm going to make it back to my house without anyone seeing me. I'm going to collect Mercy's things from upstairs and I'll be right back."

She returned with the basket Mercy had been delivered to them in, along with a quilt. She tucked the baby's bottle, formula and diapers into the basket and then tucked Mercy in, too.

Glancing around the room, she announced, "That's everything. As long as your family doesn't go into Mercy's room upstairs, they won't find any sign you've had a *bobbel* in your house."

"Denki," Turner mumbled. Tessa's whirlwind of activity caused him to recognize how devoted she was to keeping his secret. He'd never had that kind of support from a woman before except for Louisa, and if he didn't feel so debilitated, he'd probably be enthralled by her dedication.

"I don't like leaving with the fire dying out and you in such a state," she apologized, "but I know your family will take *gut* care of you. Meanwhile, rest assured I'll take *gut* care of Mercy, too."

Turner wanted to say, "I do know I can count on you, Tessa," but in his weakened condition the words came out as a groan. He'd have to tell her another time how glad he was he'd let her in on his secret and into his life.

Chapter Four

After waking up several times during the night to be sure Mercy couldn't upset the basket she was bedded in, Tessa realized if she was going to get any rest herself, she had to make other sleeping arrangements for the baby. So, on Monday she fashioned a crib by removing a deep drawer from the dresser and setting it atop Katie's old bed. She padded the bottom with a firm cushion.

Confident the sides were high enough that Mercy would be safe as well as cozy, Tessa spent the baby's nap time tending to household chores, including washing diapers. Since they'd be visible to passersby if she dried them on the clothesline with her own laundry, she pinned them to a rope she strung up in the basement. Unfortunately, they didn't dry as quickly there as they would have in the breeze, and Tessa was concerned she'd run out while waiting for them. Turner hadn't yet purchased the bird's-eye cloth Tessa asked him to buy, but she figured once he got better, she'd remind him so she could cut and stitch additional diapers.

Despite her best efforts not to entertain prying thoughts about Mercy's mother, Tessa found herself considering the baby's layette for clues. Although the *Ordnung* in their district didn't prohibit the use of disposable diapers, many Amish women preferred to use cloth. Tessa was aware a minority of *Englisch* women preferred cloth over disposables, too. So, the fact Mercy's mother included cloth diapers in the baby's basket didn't necessarily give Tessa a clue as to whether she was Amish or not. Likewise, Tessa couldn't have guessed whether Mercy's mother was *Englisch* or Amish from the pajamas and outfits she supplied, since the Amish in Willow Creek were given the option of using the same kind of clothing the *Englisch* used for their babies or else dressing them in traditional Amish attire.

"I would love to sew a little dress for you," Tessa told Mercy. The baby was lying on her tummy on a quilt on the floor, where Tessa could supervise her as Mercy used her forearms to raise her head and upper body while paddling the air with her legs like a stranded swimmer. When her strength finally ran out, her head dipped and she rubbed her face into the quilt. Tessa lifted her up and said, "But I don't know if your *mamm* is *Englisch*, and I wouldn't want to offend her by making an Amish outfit."

Mercy smiled and grabbed Tessa's prayer *kapp* strings. Tessa knew she probably held the baby more than some people would say she should, but she didn't care. As long as she gave Mercy plenty of opportunities to develop her muscles and explore her environment on her own, Tessa didn't see any harm in cuddling the child as frequently as time allowed. Mercy's expressions were simultaneously so precious and comical Tessa could have watched her for hours, whether the baby was awake or asleep. It seemed only natural to lavish her with attention and affection.

She was surprised at how quickly time passed and how content she felt staying with Mercy on Monday compared with how antsy she'd been the previous week. *Perhaps it's because I'm in my own home now, where I have plenty of chores and projects to work on when Mercy is asleep*, she mused. She even got an early start on making valentines to send to her friends and family members. Celebrating Valentine's Day by exchanging homemade cards and enjoying a special meal with friends was one of Tessa's favorite traditions, whether she had a suitor or not.

As she cut red and pink paper into the shape of hearts, she decided she ought to host a supper this year and she considered whether she should invite Turner—provided Mercy's mother had returned for her by then. He'd never accepted invitations from Katie and her before, but maybe now that he knew Tessa better he'd want to come? Then she wondered if she should make a valentine for him, too. She dithered about it as she worked, finally deciding it would be appropriate to make a simple but friendly valentine for him. But by then Mercy woke from her nap and clamored for Tessa's attention.

That evening, after she was certain Patrick and Mark had left for the day, Tessa trekked up the hill with Mercy to see how Turner was feeling. When he didn't answer the door, she let herself in.

"Turner?" She inched toward the parlor. When there was no response, she called louder, in the direction of the bedroom, "Turner, are you okay?"

In the moments before Tessa heard him

stirring, her knees went rickety and she tightened her embrace around Mercy, imagining what might have befallen Turner. Then Turner shambled into the hall, holding out his hands palms forward, like an *Englisch* police officer directing traffic.

"Please, don't *kumme* any closer. I don't want Mercy or you to catch what I have."

Noting the dark circles beneath his eyes and his pale skin, Tessa clicked her tongue against her teeth. "You still look *baremlich*," she said, before she realized it might be offensive to tell him he looked terrible. "What can I do to help? Is there anything I can get for you?"

Turner smiled weakly and said, "There's nothing I need except more rest. I honestly don't feel as bad as I look."

"It's not that you look bad, exactly," Tessa bumbled, looking for a way to smooth over her remark. "It's just that your eyes are kind of faded instead of being their usual vibrant blue."

Ach! I can't believe I just told him he has vibrant eyes, Tessa lamented. *That's more forward than telling him he looks awful!*

Turner apparently took no offense. "How has Mercy been?"

"She's been a *gut* little *haws*," Tessa gushed,

repositioning the baby to face Turner. Mercy lifted her arms and legs up and brought them down, as if jumping for joy to see him.

Turner's face brightened a little. "Did she wake up often last night?"

"*Neh*, she slept like a *bobbel*," Tessa quipped. "Which is what you ought to do, too. We'll check on you again tomorrow. I'll pray you'll feel better by then."

She was sorry they had to leave after such a short visit, but she figured the sooner Turner got to bed, the sooner he'd get well. And sure enough, when he opened the door the next evening, it was clear the rest had served him well. Turner's hair was combed, his posture was straight and, while his eyes didn't quite sparkle yet, they weren't as dull as they'd been the previous day.

"I think the worst is past, but I better not hold Mercy yet, just to be on the safe side," he said. "Funny, it's only been two days but I feel like I haven't seen her in a long time."

Moved by his affection for the baby, Tessa balanced Mercy in the crook of her arm so Turner could see her better. Mercy blinked and then tried to cram her entire fist into her mouth.

"I'm hungry, too, Mercy," Turner joked. Reaching to the top shelf of his cupboards, he pulled out two bowls. "Tessa, would you like something to eat? My appetite has returned and I'm heating a pot of the *hinkel-nudel supp* Mark brought me. His wife, Ruby, made it."

"That sounds *appenditlich*. My pantry is so depleted I thought I might have to ask Mercy if I could share her formula," Tessa cracked. Her meals for the past couple of days had consisted of buttered pasta and the leftover doughnuts Faith had given her after church.

"*Ach*, you probably haven't been able to get to the market, have you?" Turner guessed. "You've been too busy taking care of Mercy and me. I'm sorry."

"I'm not," Tessa said, peering at him longer than she meant to before glancing back down at Mercy, who was tugging her *kapp* strings again. "Besides, skipping a few meals is *gut* for my figure. It will help me lose a few pounds."

"I hardly think you need to worry about that," Turner quickly replied and Tessa wondered if he thought she was fishing for a compliment. Why did she make such superficial comments around him? He continued, "You're *wilkom* to anything in my cupboards. I've got plenty of—"

"*Neh, neh,*" Tessa said with a giggle, her embarrassment forgotten. "I appreciate the offer but I'm not going to do my grocery shopping in your pantry! I'm fine. Tomorrow night Katie and a few friends are coming for our Wednesday night supper and it's Katie's turn to bring the meal, so I'll be all set. That is, if you're well enough by then to look after Mercy for a few hours?"

"I'll be well enough. I plan to return to work tomorrow."

"Are you sure you're up to that? You're still on the mend." Even as she asked the question, Tessa realized how much she sounded like her mother. "I'm sorry. I'm clucking like a nervous hen, aren't I?"

Turner chuckled. "No need to apologize. You're much more considerate of my health than I've been about your daily errands. If you'll let me, on Thursday afternoon I'll give you a ride to wherever you need to go."

"What about Mercy?"

Turner lifted his shoulders. "We'll only be gone an hour or so. She'll be fine on her own, won't she?"

Tessa's mouth fell open. Then she saw the glint in his eye: he was teasing. No-nonsense Turner King had actually made a joke. "Oh, you!"

"Mercy will *kumme* with us, of course," he said. "We'll wait for you in the buggy while you make your purchases. I have to pick up a few parts in Highland Springs, but afterward I'll swing back to Willow Creek and take you to the market before it closes."

Usually, Tessa shopped at the market on Main Street, which she could have walked to, but suddenly she didn't want to pass up the chance to spend more time with Turner. Remembering they needed diaper cloth for Mercy, she suggested she and the baby could accompany him to Highland Springs. That way, he could accomplish his business errand and she could go to the *Englisch* fabric store there and shop at the *Englisch* supermarket all in the same trip.

"That's a great idea," Turner agreed. "Now, let's eat."

As Tessa sipped her soup, it occurred to her that although she never especially liked grocery shopping, this time she was looking forward to it every bit as much as gathering with her sister and friends on Wednesday evening.

Because Tessa had taken all of the formula to the *daadi haus* and the baby was getting cranky, she and Mercy left right after Tessa finished eating. Turner piled the bowls in the sink, heated water for tea and ambled over to sit on the sofa, but he was too jittery to stay seated. He wandered onto the porch with his mug and looked up at the stars. Reflecting on the past few days, he realized his illness had been a blessing in disguise in more ways than one. Not only had it given him a legitimate reason for missing church services, but the virus had hit him so hard he hadn't had any ability to worry or wonder about Jacqueline. Nor had he had the wherewithal to pray. But now that he was feeling better, he said, "*Denki*, Lord Jesus, for healing me and for sparing Mercy and Tessa from the flu. *Denki* for using my illness to show me my limitations, even if they're difficult to face. Help me to lean on You for guidance, not on my efforts alone. And if it's Your will, please return Jacqueline to us soon."

As he slowly drank the rest of his tea, he thought about what he could do to show Tessa how much he valued her help, especially while he was sick. He considered paying her a salary in addition to waiving her rent, but he sensed she would be insulted by the gesture. No, he wanted to demonstrate his appreciation in a more personal way, but he didn't know what kind of gift she might like. He didn't even know if a gift would be welcome. Having limited experience in relationships with women, he didn't want to risk making her feel offended or uncomfortable.

Perhaps he could take her to supper after they completed their errands in Highland Springs. Tessa said she disliked cooking, but eating was a necessity, so it wasn't as if he'd be crossing a line by inviting her to have supper with him in a public place. Yes, that's what he'd do. He felt another surge of energy, and he hummed as he went inside and washed the dishes. Then he looked around the parlor and decided it needed tidying, too. By the time he had finished, he felt drained again, but as he lay in bed he realized he'd spent the last hour thinking about something other than his sister's predicament and he didn't even feel guilty. He felt… He felt *hopeful*. With a smile curling his lips, he fell into a sound sleep.

The next day when Turner arrived at the shop, Mark asked how he felt.

"*Gut*. Like a new man."

"Ruby's *supp* has that effect on me, too," Mark said and Turner grinned. It wasn't the soup he was thinking about; it was *sharing* the soup with Tessa.

He smiled again later that afternoon when Tessa and Mercy arrived at his house. He took the basket from Tessa with one hand and held the door open with the other.

"Look at you!" Tessa exclaimed. "I guess you were ready to go back to work after all—your eyes are absolutely luminous today."

Turner was glad she immediately began unpacking Mercy's things from the large canvas tote bag and didn't notice if his ears were as red as they felt. Was she complimenting his eyes? No woman had commented on his appearance like that before, so he wasn't sure whether to say thank you or not. "What has this *kind* been eating?" he asked, picking up Mercy and weighing her in one hand. "She seems twice as heavy as she was a few days ago."

Mercy cooed at him and he kissed the top of her head, which smelled like lavender; it smelled like Tessa.

"She's been smiling ever since she woke from her nap," Tessa said. "She must be happy she gets to stay at your house with you again."

But Tessa wasn't out the door for more than twenty seconds before Mercy started to snivel. Turner rocked from side to side, trying to pacify her. "It's all right, Mercy. Tessa will be back again soon," he said. Turner's words didn't have any effect on Mercy's whimpering, but they sure made him feel happy.

After Faith, Anna, Katie and Tessa finished eating the yumasetta casserole Katie prepared, along with the marinated carrots and peas Anna brought, they did the dishes and tidied the kitchen together. Then Faith brought out her famous apple fry pies.

"Let's have these in the parlor with tea," Katie suggested.

Wiping her hands on her apron, Tessa replied, "I'm afraid I don't have any tea."

"That's okay. They go just as well with milk."

"I haven't got milk, either."

"No tea and no milk?" Katie shook her head and pulled open the pantry door. "Look, there's nothing in here except a can of soup and half a box of noodles! You call that a pantry? Honestly, Tessa, sometimes I worry about you."

Tessa snorted. "You remind me of *Mamm.* I'm sorry, but I didn't get around to shopping yet this week."

"How could you 'not get around' to shopping for food?" Katie squinted at her. When Tessa didn't respond, she said, "You aren't working at Schrock's, so how have you been spending your days?"

"I'm not sure that's your concern," Tessa replied, "but I've been giving the house a thorough cleaning and catching up on projects I didn't do when I was working."

Apparently, Faith and Anna sensed the hint of tension because they casually moved into the parlor. It was unusual for the Fisher sisters to argue, especially in front of anyone else. Tessa pulled four small dishes from the cupboard, keeping her back to her sister as she placed the fry pies on the plates.

"I'm not as irresponsible as you think I am," she said. *If you only knew how I'd spent my week, you'd understand why I didn't go shopping.*

"I didn't say you're irresponsible," Katie protested. A long silence followed until she said, "Now that I look around, I can see how much work you've been doing. The floors never shone like this when I lived here and they still don't in my new house. I asked how you're spending your days because I worry you're lonely. I understand you like living alone—but being alone all day? That's not like you. You've got such a social personality I was afraid you were… I don't know, depressed or something, now that you're not working in town. I'm also worried you might not have enough money for groceries. Mason and I can help you if—"

"Lappich gans!" Tessa called Katie a silly goose before pulling a tin from the back of the cupboard. She pried off the top and showed its contents to her sister. "See? I have plenty of money. But I appreciate your offer anyway, dear sister."

The pair spontaneously embraced, their rift mended as quickly as it had begun. "I'm glad you're managing financially," Katie said over Tessa's shoulder. "But I know you well enough to know you need daily interaction with others. What are you doing for fellowship? What are you doing for *schpass*?"

Tessa didn't know if caring for Mercy could be considered "fun," and she couldn't have told Katie about it even if she did, so instead she answered her sister's question by saying, "For *schpass*, I'm planning a potluck supper with you and Faith and Anna. *Kumme*, let's eat dessert."

They carried the fry pies to their friends waiting in the parlor, but Anna declined, saying she felt a bit nauseated. Then she patted her stomach. "Besides, my tummy is going to be big enough in a few months' time as it is."

Usually the Amish didn't discuss their

pregnancies, sometimes not even publicly acknowledging they were expecting until the baby was born. But Katie and Tessa had been tight friends with Anna since they moved to Willow Creek, and they'd recently gotten to know Faith better, too, since she was Katie's sister-in-law. Because neither Anna nor Faith had sisters of their own, the four young women gathered on sister days for quilting, canning, gardening and other projects. Chatting as they worked, they sometimes confided news about their lives they wouldn't necessarily share with others.

"That's *wunderbaar*!" Faith leaned over and squeezed her friend's arm.

"Wunderbaar!" Katie echoed.

"What a blessing!" Tessa exclaimed. "You're going to love cuddling the *bobbel*, feeding her, watching her sleep… Wait until the first time she smiles because she recognizes you've *kumme* into the room. It will melt your heart."

Tessa didn't realize she was crooking her arm the way she did when she held Mercy until Anna replied, "Look at you! You seem as excited about motherhood as I am."

"Neh, not Tessa," Faith objected. "She likes living alone and working at Schrock's too much to ever get married and become a *mamm*. Right, Tessa?"

Unlike the *Englisch*, most Amish women gave up their jobs outside their homes once they got married, and virtually all of them quit working when their babies were born. Some mothers later returned to work in their family businesses, but not until their children were much older, and even then they kept their offspring close by. Faith understood better than anyone the appeal of being a single Amish woman living alone and working outside her home because she'd done it herself for a year before getting married. So Tessa knew her remark wasn't meant as criticism, but she felt prickled all the same. *It's not that I've changed my mind about my plans, but who's to say I won't at some point?* It was a peculiar thought for her to have, considering all she was doing in order to keep her current living situation as it was.

"Well, that might be true right now, but..." she mumbled.

"But first she has to meet a suitor worthy of her devotion," Katie finished for her. "Which is part of the reason we wanted you to join us for supper tonight."

Even in front of her close friends, Tessa was mortified. "I only agreed to host a potluck supper. Don't go planting any celery just yet," she said, referring to the Amish tradition of growing large amounts of the vegetable prior to a wedding. Celery was a main ingredient in many of the wedding dishes, and it was also used to decorate the tables.

As Katie elaborated on their plan to host a potluck and invite David to attend, Tessa could hardly concentrate. She kept watching the clock, hoping there would be time to check in on Mercy before Turner put her down for the night. But her sister and friends were so excited about the prospect of matching Tessa and David on Saturday when he was in town again, they schemed until nine o'clock, and by then, the baby was undoubtedly asleep. After closing the door behind her guests, Tessa headed straight for bed, where she dozed off thinking, *I'm only a night's slumber away from seeing Mercy again. And Turner, too.*

Turner panicked when he heard a knock on the door at seven twenty in the morning. Tessa usually didn't arrive until seven forty-five. Mercy was burbling happily but loudly in the parlor; if Mark or Patrick were on his doorstep, they'd be bound to hear her. He cracked the door partway.

"Guder mariye," Tessa said.

She must smile from the moment she

wakes up, he thought and beamed at her in return, opening the door wider to let her in. "I thought you were Patrick or Mark," he explained.

"Neh," she teased. "They're taller and they have beards."

Turner laughed. "What brings you here so early? Is something wrong?" Despite her sunny appearance, he suddenly worried she might have come to tell him she was ill and couldn't take care of Mercy today—or go out shopping tonight.

"Neh, nothing's wrong at all. I came early to ask if perhaps I could watch Mercy at the *daadi haus* instead of up here from now on. That way, while Mercy is sleeping I can keep up with my household projects, as well as wash her *windle*."

Turner hesitated. He understood why Tessa would want to spend the day in her own home instead of his, but he was afraid someone—like a suitor—might visit her unexpectedly.

As if aware of his concerns, Tessa continued, "I'm quite certain no one will stop by. Katie's at school all day, Faith is working in the bakery and Anna's focus isn't on socializing right now. My parents wouldn't come all the way from Shady Valley without telling me in advance. At least, not on a weekday."

"But what if I need to work later than usual, into the evening hours?"

"Katie, Faith and Anna will be preparing their suppers in the evening, so they're even less likely to visit."

Turner realized he was going to have to be more direct with Tessa. "But what if your... your suitor decides to surprise you with a visit some evening?"

"That *would* be a surprise," Tessa said and Turner's mouth drooped, until she continued, "since I don't have a suitor."

"Gut!" he exclaimed and then lowered his voice, stammering, "I—I mean, it's *gut* that no one will be stopping by. *Jah*, it's fine to watch Mercy at your house."

Tessa clapped vivaciously. *"Wunderbaar.* I'll load up the basket with her things and then return for her in a minute."

"Don't be *lecherich.* I'll carry Mercy's basket and walk down with you."

Turner felt so vibrant he could have bounded down the hill in three steps. When Tessa and Mercy were settled into the *daadi haus*, Turner reminded Tessa, "I'll stop in at about three o'clock to take you to Highland Springs."

"We'll be ready and waiting, won't we, Mercy?" Tessa asked and Mercy gave a gleeful squawk.

"I'll take that to mean *jah*," Turner said, tickling the underside of the baby's chin.

He didn't stop whistling all morning, and during their lunch break, Patrick asked, "What's your secret, Turner?"

Turner was devouring his bologna sandwich and nearly choked as he tried to swallow. "What secret?"

"You've been grinning ear to ear all morning, you did more of the wheel assembly than you'd planned and you're wolfing down that lunch like you've never eaten before. Usually when people have been ill, it takes a while for them to get back to their previous state of health and mind. But you seem to have bounced back even better than you were before."

Turner was relieved: Patrick didn't know anything about his secret. He lifted his shoulders and turned his hands palms up. "I suppose I'm blessed," he said before taking another big bite of bread.

"Well, it's *gut* that you're feeling so much better, since you'll be on your own in the shop on Saturday."

Turner had forgotten both of his brothers were traveling to their in-laws' houses for a long weekend, but the reminder filled him with relief. He had planned to see if he and

Tessa could somehow take turns caring for Mercy while the other one was at their family's home worship service, since it would be an off Sunday this week. Now he wouldn't have to inconvenience her or ask his family to change their worship time. As for manning the shop on Saturday, that was an impossibility since Tessa would be working and Turner couldn't bring Mercy with him. But keeping it open on a Saturday wasn't an absolute requirement and, as long as all the urgent repairs were completed, his brothers wouldn't be any wiser if the shop stayed closed.

Turner's industriousness didn't wane throughout the afternoon; if anything, he became more enlivened as he worked. By the time he told his brothers he was leaving to pick up the parts for Jonas's buggy in Highland Springs, he had to keep himself from charging out the door. He strode toward his house where he washed his hands and face and put on a clean shirt Barbara Verkler had washed for him, and then he hitched the horse and started down the lane.

Turner's house and the *daadi haus* were separated from the workshop by both distance and a thick stand of trees, but to be safe Turner and Tessa agreed she'd carry the baby outside in the basket, shielding Mercy from view with a light blanket. Their plan was for Tessa to sit with Mercy in the back of the buggy, where they wouldn't be plainly seen if they happened to pass other buggies.

Concerned Mercy would be bothered by the noise of the buggy's wheels on the road and the motion of the carriage as they traveled, Turner paid special attention to how he handled the horse. As it turned out, the rhythmic motion and sound of the horse's gait put Mercy to sleep, so Turner and Tessa didn't converse during the trip to the salvage yard, nor from the salvage yard to the supermarket.

"I won't be long," Tessa whispered as she stepped down from the buggy.

"Take your time," Turner insisted.

But she was quick to return with a cart full of food items for herself and more formula for Mercy. After that, they stopped at a mini-mall so she could purchase bird's-eye cotton from the fabric store. Turner's palms went clammy as she climbed into the carriage the final time. Traffic was heavy this time of day and it wouldn't be easy to change direction once they were on their way. He had to ask her now.

Since Mercy was still asleep, he spoke in a low voice, woodenly reciting the words he'd rehearsed while she was in the store. "If you're hungry, I'd like to treat you to supper so you don't have to wait until we get back to eat. I've heard the Pasta Palace is a *gut* restaurant."

The parking-lot lights were bright enough that Turner could see Tessa biting her lip. Was she trying not to laugh or was she honestly considering his invitation?

"*Denki*, that's very kind of you," she hemmed. "I just, um…"

Turner could have crawled into a hole. It was clear she was trying to drum up an excuse not to accept his offer. He had been foolish to think she might want to spend time socializing with him. She and her friends were probably going to share a good chuckle over this. "If you'd rather not, that's fine," he said. "I only figured we could avoid the *Englisch* rush-hour traffic if we delayed our return to Willow Creek."

"*Neh*, it's not that I don't want to eat supper with you," she protested. "It's a very thoughtful offer. It's just that I… I've been eating nothing but pasta for the past four days and I'm not sure I could swallow another bite of it."

Turner's morale soared. "Of course you can't," he said. "I should have asked you what kind of meal you'd prefer. Where would you like to go instead?"

They agreed on an American diner, where they both ordered Philly cheesesteak sandwiches and french fries. While they were waiting for their food to arrive, Mercy stirred in Tessa's arms. Squinting one eye open, the baby stretched and yawned and then closed her eye again before struggling to open both eyes. When she did, she blinked as if to ask, "Where am I?" Watching her, Tessa and Turner both chuckled. Within minutes, she was as alert as could be, reaching for the utensils and kicking at the table, gurgling or making an ooh sound. She was clearly enjoying the new environment and being the focus of Tessa's and Turner's undivided attention.

"How old is your baby?" the waitress asked when she brought their order to the table.

Turner's heart skipped a beat as he waited for Tessa's reply, but she nonchalantly answered, "A little over three months," without clarifying that Mercy wasn't her child.

"She takes after her dad—she's got his big blue eyes. Adorable," the server said, and Turner felt as if he couldn't breathe. If the woman noticed their family resemblance at a glance, Tessa undoubtedly had seen it, too.

"At least she doesn't have my nose," Tessa

nonchalantly quipped, but the waitress had already turned away and didn't hear the remark.

After he said grace, Turner hesitated to raise his head and look at Tessa. His cheeks and forehead were burning, as well as his ears. Tessa had never let on if she thought Mercy was his child, but then again she hadn't asked any questions about Mercy's mother, either. Maybe she'd noticed the resemblance and assumed Mercy was his all along. For reasons he couldn't explain, Turner felt compelled to make sure Tessa knew he wasn't Mercy's father. It was embarrassing to even bring up the topic, but he had to set the record straight.

He cleared his throat and said quietly, "Mercy isn't my *dochder*."

Tessa pulled the wrapper off her straw and casually replied, "She isn't mine, either, but we couldn't let the waitress know that, could we?"

Tessa's lighthearted response filled Turner with such warmth he felt like leaping across the table and embracing her and Mercy both. Instead he replied, "*Neh*, we couldn't." He paused to catch her eye before adding, "Although if you were her *mamm*, I think she'd be fortunate to inherit your nose. You have an elegant profile."

"Denki," Tessa murmured, dipping her head as she dabbed a french fry into a little pool of ketchup.

Switching the subject, Turner said, "I'm often taken aback by the comments *Englischers* make, but it doesn't seem to bother you."

Tessa shrugged. "I used to be uncomfortable having conversations with them when I first started working at Schrock's. I was always on edge, afraid they'd ask something too intrusive and I wouldn't know how to respond. But then I realized they're just curious about me. Or about the Amish way of life. They intend no harm. And sometimes they even mean to be complimentary, like that waitress."

Turner was skeptical. "Their questions don't nettle you at all?"

"On occasion, *jah*. But when that happens, I switch the topic or respond with a curt but congenial reply. Or else I meet their remark with silence, just like I would when an Amish acquaintance asks a question I consider nosy or inappropriate. Besides, some of the *Englisch* believe in *Gott* and it's interesting to hear them talk about their beliefs, even if they have a different way of living out their Christian faith than we do."

When Tessa put it that way, Turner realized she wasn't being naïve; in fact, she had more wisdom—and charitableness—than he did. He still might not trust most *Englischers*, but his confidence in Tessa was growing by the hour.

Chapter Five

Once again on Saturday there was a long line of customers at Schrock's, some of whom were unusually ill-mannered.

One woman barked at Tessa for giving her the wrong change. When she slapped the money on the counter and demanded Tessa recount it, Tessa obliged, proving she'd given the woman the correct amount due her. The customer then swept the money from the counter, shoved it in her purse and walked away without a word of apology. Another customer toppled a box of candles, and someone else allowed his child to handle one of the wooden tractors while sucking a fat lollipop. When the father was finished browsing, he set the sticky toy back on the shelf, which caused the child to scream and kick until the father promised him a chocolate milkshake at lunch.

"Tessa, you must have nerves of steel not to be fazed by the rush of customers," Joseph commented during a quiet spell. "I appreciate how patient you've been this morning."

"It's my pleasure," Tessa said.

Everything was Tessa's pleasure that day, primarily because the evening before last Turner had told her she had an elegant profile. Tessa wasn't ordinarily given to thoughts about her appearance, as she knew vanity was a sin, but if there was one physical feature she used to wish she could change, it was her nose.

As a girl, she wasn't even aware she had a prominent nose until a classmate told her it stuck out like a chicken's beak. After that she became self-conscious and frequently stole away to her family's washroom to angle a hand mirror against the mirror above the sink so she could study her nose from the side. Tessa had realized she was being vain, just as she had realized she was growing envious of all the girls at school who had little round noses. But one day when the same boy repeatedly called her "Beaky" under his breath, Tessa asked to be excused. She told the teacher she felt sick, which meant she was lying in addition to being envious and vain. Wracked with guilt, she hid behind a tree in the schoolyard and cried until school let out and Katie walked her home.

"The Lord gave you a nose just like your *daed*'s, and I think it makes him look distinctive," her mother had said when Tessa finally confessed what had happened. "One day someone will think the same way about you. But it's more important to focus on what's in someone's heart than what's on someone's face. Now dry your eyes and help me peel these potatoes for supper."

As Tessa had matured, she was able to brush it off when others commented on the size or shape of her nose until her first suitor asked her, without a hint of derision, how she'd broken it.

"I've never broken my nose!" she'd declared.

The young man had appeared mortified. "I'm sorry. I just assumed…"

Although he hadn't meant to be insulting, Tessa had been offended all the same. So she was delighted when Turner said he liked the very thing about her face other people considered unattractive or peculiar. More than that, she was euphoric Turner was so chivalrous as to treat her to supper, knowing how hungry she'd be if she waited until they returned home to eat.

Far from feeling at a loss for what to discuss during their meal, Tessa had been utterly engaged in conversation with him. Like other young men she knew, Turner talked about buggies, but his emphasis wasn't on the vehicle as a prized possession but on his work at the shop. A spark lit his eyes when he gave examples of the challenges he and his brothers encountered, both with repairs and with their customers. As he spoke, his facial muscles visually relaxed and he leaned back against the booth seat, occasionally using his hands to illustrate an anecdote. It was clear he found his profession fulfilling. Tessa could have listened to his resonant voice all evening, but he was careful not to monopolize the conversation, and asked about her family and clerking at Schrock's. Since Mercy was so content, they took their time eating, lingering over a banana split for dessert, which they shared.

As Tessa reflected on that evening, she couldn't help humming, and the afternoon sailed by even quicker than the morning. When Joseph locked the door behind the final customer, Tessa worked with unusual efficiency to perform the chores that needed to be completed before she left. *The sooner I get home and eat, the sooner I'll be able to visit Mercy and Turner,* she thought.

Tessa was putting a new bag in the trash bin when Joseph invited her to join his family for supper that evening. Usually, she'd jump at the chance to eat one of Amity's delicious meals and spend the evening playing board games with their rambunctious young brood, but tonight Tessa racked her brain for a polite yet truthful way to decline Joseph's offer. Then it hit her like a bolt of lightning: tonight she was hosting the potluck supper. In her giddiness over her evening out with Turner, she'd completely forgotten about the party.

"*Denki,* I would like to but I can't. I'm hosting guests at my house tonight."

"Ah well, perhaps another time," Joseph said. "I'll finish up here since I have to wait for Amity and the *kinner* to pick me up. You can go ahead and go home. Bundle up. It looks like it's snowing again."

Exiting through the back door, Tessa regretted that she hadn't worn her heavier cloak and a scarf when she'd left the house that morning. For a few seconds, she hoped the bad weather might prevent her guests from coming so she could visit Turner and Mercy instead, but she knew that was improbable.

The snow was fluffy, not heavy, and even if it kept up, her sister and friends could easily transverse the roads by horse and buggy.

She'd made her way down the back alley and was nearing the parking lot behind the mercantile that was used by cars as well as buggies, when she looked up and noticed a figure waving at her.

"Tessa!" the man called.

As he passed beneath the street lamp, she could see it was Jeremy. Tessa momentarily stopped cold in her tracks before hugging her cloak to her chest and sidestepping him. She didn't have time for his antics. "I'm in a hurry, Jeremy. I need to get home. Excuse me."

"Please wait," Jeremy said, following at her elbow. "I'm not going to make a spectacle of myself again. I want to apologize to you for my behavior last week. I'm very sorry. There's no excuse for my behavior, and it doesn't reflect the respect I have for you and your beliefs. I hope in time you'll forgive me."

Tessa stopped to face him. She was shivering but she wanted to look Jeremy in the eyes. She knew it took humility and courage for him to apologize. "I forgive you, Jeremy."

Jeremy's voice squeaked as he said, "Thank you, Tessa. That means a lot to me."

She nodded. "I really do have to go now—"

"Do you want a ride?" Jeremy offered. "You look cold and you said you're in a hurry. My sister Donna is in the car waiting for me."

Tessa hesitated. The Amish were permitted to accept rides in cars from the *Englisch* and she still had to tidy the house before the guests arrived. She didn't want Jeremy to doubt she was sincere about accepting his apology, and since his sister—who had given Tessa rides in the past—would be traveling with them, she didn't have to worry about the impropriety of riding alone with an *Englisch* man. But Turner had indicated Jeremy wasn't welcome on the property without an invitation from him, and Tessa wanted to respect his wishes.

"That's okay, I'll walk." Her bare fingertips were going numb.

"I can drop you off at the end of your driveway, since I haven't had a chance to apologize to your landlord yet and I know he doesn't want me around."

This time, Tessa didn't refuse. She scurried with him across the parking lot to his car. Since his back seat was stacked with oversize boxes of paper goods for the restaurant, she slid into the front seat next to Donna, who gave her an enthusiastic greeting and scooted closer to her brother. Jeremy had left the car running and the interior was toasty warm. Because she'd accepted a ride, Tessa figured she'd have enough time to prepare lemon squares for the party; they were her specialty, the one dessert she never burned or undercooked. She had forgotten to tell Turner about the potluck, but maybe before everyone arrived she'd run up to his place with a plate of lemon squares for him, too.

Turner stepped down and paced the length of his horse and buggy where he'd parked it in the lot behind the mercantile. Taking several deep breaths, he tried to gather his thoughts. The day had started off so well, with Mercy waking in a pleasant mood, smiling at Turner when he changed her and listening raptly whenever he carried her to the window and pointed out the snowflakes. He knew she probably couldn't understand him, but he was delighted that she seemed enthralled with the sound of his voice.

Still, after spending all day indoors Turner began to feel confined, which made him appreciate Tessa's help all the more. Wanting to be as considerate of her as she'd been to him, he decided to pick her up after work so she wouldn't have to walk home in the cold. He planned to ask if she wanted to share a pizza, which they could pick up on the other side of town and then eat at his house.

Figuring he'd catch Tessa coming down the alley behind Main Street, Turner headed toward the parking lot behind the mercantile to watch for her. Rounding the corner, he spotted her beneath a street lamp. But instead of walking toward home, Tessa was getting into a car. He knew that car; it was Jeremy's. Sure enough, he spotted Jeremy just as he opened the door to get in on the driver's side. Turner pulled into the parking lot entrance as Jeremy's car was driving out the exit at the opposite end.

Now, stomping back and forth next to his buggy, Turner tried to make sense of why he felt so irked. Tessa technically wasn't doing anything wrong; she was probably only getting a lift home. But it seemed inappropriate for her to accept a ride alone with an *Englisch* man. Didn't she know that people might gossip? Turner had come to believe she had more discretion and exercised sounder judgment than that, but apparently he was mistaken. Furthermore, Tessa had heard him tell Jeremy he wasn't welcome on the property without an invitation from Turner. Didn't she have any regard for Turner's wishes?

Suddenly a voice behind him said, "Hello, Turner."

Turner was so lost in thought he hadn't noticed anyone approach the lot. "Hello, Joseph." He fiddled with the horse's reins, as if that were the reason he was idling in the parking lot. "You can't be too careful in this weather."

"*Jah*, that's true," Joseph agreed. "You know, I'm glad our paths crossed. Amity and I were just saying we don't get to see you nearly as often as we'd like to. We hope you'll call on us soon."

"*Denki* for the invitation." Turner kept his response neutral. He felt deceptive enough pretending to adjust a rein that didn't need adjusting; he wasn't going to make false promises to Joseph, too.

Just then Turner heard a faint whining. During the past week or so his ears had grown finely attuned to the sound: it meant Mercy was waking up. In a matter of two minutes, she might start wailing her lungs out. Turner wanted to skedaddle before Joseph heard her, but it was too late.

"Do you hear a cat?" he asked.

Turner cocked his head as if listening.

"*Neh*, I don't hear a cat" was all he could truthfully say. Fortunately, Joseph's wife turned down the alley and the buggy made enough noise to drown out Mercy's mewling.

"I see Amity is here to pick you up," Turner commented. "Better not delay. With the way the *Englisch* drive in snow, it's best to get off the roads as soon as possible."

Joseph chuckled as he headed toward his family's buggy. "We'll see you around soon, I hope."

"*Gut nacht*, Joseph." Turner said loudly, hoping his voice blocked out the sound of Mercy's.

As soon as he climbed into the buggy and spoke sweet nothings to Mercy, she quieted. And when the horse trotted back toward home, she sounded out, "Aah," holding the syllable for a long time before repeating it as if it were a song. Turner, however, was far from singing. Rattled that his secret had nearly been exposed, he kneaded the muscle in his neck, which was tighter than it had been since before he'd gotten ill.

Because his plans for the evening were ruined anyway and Mercy seemed satisfied to be nestled in her basket in the back, Turner decided to stop at the phone shanty. He situated his buggy so it obscured him and Mercy from view, lest any other buggies pass by. It had been weeks since he'd spoken to Louisa and, although it was unlikely, he hoped she might know more about Jacqueline's current situation than he did. He could usually count on a teenager to pick up the phone at this time on a Saturday and today was no exception.

"You must be very quiet," Turner said to Mercy as he waited for the girl who answered the phone in Ohio to fetch Louisa from her house close by. The phone shanty Turner used was enclosed on three sides, more like a booth than a room, and Turner held Mercy in a seated position with her back to his chest, the way he'd seen Tessa do it. Tessa had crocheted a pink cap for the baby, and she was wearing it now. Snuggled in Turner's arms, Mercy was content to watch the snowflakes as he wiggled her up and down.

After exchanging brief pleasantries, Louisa said, "I'm afraid I've heard disturbing news. Remember I told you an acquaintance of Jacqueline's recently said her cousin in Elmsville told her about an Amish *maedel* who ran away with an *Englischer* during her *rumspringa* and now works in a convenience store near Willow Creek?"

"Jah." Of course Turner remembered; that's why he'd been searching the markets

in his area. He sensed Louisa was reluctant to report whatever new information she'd heard.

"I'm sorry to tell you this, Turner, but the *maedel* supposedly gave birth to a *bobbel*."

Louisa's news would have shattered him, had Turner not already known about it. Although he felt guilty because Louisa was clearly in anguish over the rumor, Turner didn't confirm what he knew. He couldn't, not when Jacqueline had asked him not to.

It sounded as if Louisa was sniffing. Turner had always known his aunt cared deeply for Jacqueline, but he'd been so absorbed by his own concerns he hadn't fully considered that Louisa felt like a mother to the young girl. She was probably as grieved by this news as he had been. On top of that, her husband was ailing after suffering a series of small strokes, so she was worried about him, too. Turner tried to think of something to say to console her.

"As devastating as it would be if Jacqueline bore a *bobbel*, if the rumor is true at least we'd know she was still alive," he said. Turner had never allowed himself to hint at his deepest fear until now. Soothed by Mercy's presence, he added, "At least we'd still have hope she might one day return to us."

"*Jah*, that is our prayer." Louisa continued

slowly, "But supposedly this *maedel* is considering leaving the Amish altogether. The *bobbel*'s *daed* is a *kind* himself and doesn't want anything to do with the *bobbel* or with her. It's said she's thinking of moving out of the region altogether. Maybe even giving up her *bobbel*."

Turner's legs were jelly. Jacqueline wasn't going to return? She was going to leave Mercy behind? The possibility caused his throat to burn and his lungs to constrict. He couldn't fathom how Jacqueline could even contemplate leaving Mercy behind permanently. Just then the baby grunted and kicked her legs to let Turner know he'd stopped bouncing her and she wanted to keep moving. He automatically complied.

"Turner?" Louisa was prompting him from his silence. "You know how rumors start in small communities. This one could be completely false. Or perhaps it's not about Jacqueline at all."

"Perhaps not," Turner managed to say. He pressed Louisa for more details about who Jacqueline's acquaintances heard the rumor from; maybe he could track the person down and ask more questions. But apparently the gossip had been passed along so many times, even those repeating it weren't sure where it originated. Turner finally bade Louisa good-night and then he and Mercy continued on their way. When he pulled up the lane to his house, he didn't notice whether Jeremy's car was at Tessa's. He had far more pressing things on his mind.

Tessa was concerned when she looked out Katie's window and didn't see a lamp on at Turner's house. Was he napping because he felt ill again? Tessa's guests would be there within the hour and her dessert was still baking, but she darted up the hill and rapped on Turner's door. There was no answer so she knocked again, loud enough to wake Mercy from the soundest slumber, but there was still no stirring within the house. She sped to the stable. Pulling the door open, she saw the horse and buggy weren't there. Where could Turner and Mercy have gone?

Making a mental list of Mercy's supplies, Tessa tried to determine if Turner urgently needed to purchase something for the baby. But even if he did, Turner wouldn't have gone into a store alone with Mercy. Tessa wondered if he took the baby for a ride in the buggy to calm her, since it had had a tranquilizing effect on her on Thursday. But it was unlikely he'd have gone out with Mercy on a snowy evening—unless something was wrong with the baby and he needed help. A dozen scenarios flitted through Tessa's mind, each one more disturbing than the first.

As concerned as she was, Tessa realized even if something upsetting had befallen Turner or Mercy, there was nothing she could do about it now except pray. Once she was home, she bowed her head and beseeched the Lord, "Heavenly Father, please keep Turner and Mercy healthy and safe, wherever they are, and bring them home soon."

By the time she'd pulled the lemon squares out of the oven and slid the corn bread muffins onto the rack in their place, her guests had arrived. To Tessa's dismay, in addition to the married couples, there were two single men, but no other single female guests present. Hunter and Faith brought David, the widower, who was short and portly and wore glasses. Anna and Fletcher brought a tall, muscular young man with sandy-blond hair named Jonah, who just moved to Willow Creek from Ohio to work on Fletcher's carpentry crew. After introductions were made and the men stamped off their boots and were settled in the parlor, the women retreated to the kitchen to tend to a few last-minute food preparations.

"I'm sorry, Tessa," Anna whispered. "I invited the daughter of my stepmother's childhood friend who is visiting her from out of state, but the entire household, including their guests, came down with that nasty stomach bug that's been going around."

Recalling how sick Turner had been, Tessa sympathized, "That's too bad she's ill, but I understand. *Kumme*, let's go play a round of charades while the corn bread bakes and Katie's chili simmers."

The group broke into two teams: David, Tessa, Jonah and Faith against the others. Every player jotted the name of a person from the Bible on slips of paper, and then the two teams exchanged the slips. The teams took turns and each person had two minutes to act out the character they'd chosen; if their team guessed it before the timer went off, they scored a point.

When it was Tessa's turn, she chose a slip that said Queen Esther. As she pretended to don a crown, Jonah and Faith called out the names of every king and ruler they could imagine. King David. Saul. Caesar. Nebuchadnezzar. Each time Tessa vigorously shook her head no, Faith's and Jonah's subsequent answers grew louder and more urgent as they attempted to guess the correct person. Tessa continued to mime Esther praying, fasting and preparing a banquet for the king. By this time, Jonah and Faith were both standing as well as shouting, whereas David was silent and immobile, a blank look on his face.

"It's Cain, preparing stew!" Jonah yelled.

"Cain wasn't a king," Faith said with animated disgust.

Tessa was so exasperated they assumed she was a male that she threw her hands in the air and grimaced exaggeratedly at them to indicate they were on the wrong track.

"You're Moses and you're frustrated with the Israelites' idol worship!" Faith said loudly, interpreting her gesture to be part of the game. The other team realized Tessa hadn't been acting out a role, and they all cracked up at Faith for continuing to guess who Tessa was imitating. Tessa laughed so hard she bent over, clutching her stomach.

As the timer sounded, Jonah hollered triumphantly, "You're King Solomon falling on his sword! Am I right? Did I guess it? I'm right, aren't I?"

Tessa was too breathless to reply and the others howled with amusement. When the rumpus subsided, Tessa good-naturedly groaned. "Neither of you really had any idea who I was?" she asked Faith and Jonah.

"*Neh*, but at least we were guessing," Faith said, zestfully chastising David. "One of our team members didn't say a word."

"I thought perhaps she was being Queen Esther," David replied, eliciting a cheer from Tessa.

"I was! Why didn't you call it out?"

David's shrug caused Tessa to wonder whether he was incredibly self-conscious or just bored with their game. Either way, his reservation didn't bode well for them being a match; humor was important to Tessa. Until she played charades with her friends, she hadn't realized how long it had been since she'd had a good, hard belly laugh herself. She'd missed that.

"Do I smell something burning?" Hunter interrupted her thoughts.

"*Ach*, my corn bread!" Tessa yelped. Acrid smoke filled the air after she darted into the kitchen and removed the charred muffins from the oven. But when everyone gathered around the table, they politely ignored the thin blue haze hanging overhead.

"Sorry about that," Tessa said, utterly chagrined. "My *mamm* says I'd forget my own head sometimes and I'm afraid it's true."

"That's okay," David consoled her. "My Charity frequently does the same thing herself."

"Who's Charity, your wife?" Jonah asked.

"*Neh*, my daughter. She's eleven," David replied.

Tessa cringed to hear her skills being compared to those of a girl eleven years of age, but David continued obliviously. "Most of the time she's done a *wunderbaar* job preparing our meals ever since my wife passed on, although there have been a few mishaps. I'm sure with a little more female guidance Charity will grow to be a fine cook."

Could it be any more obvious he's looking for a wife? Tessa wondered. David might have expressed such a sentiment subtly to Tessa in private if he wanted to court her, in order to gauge her interest in him by how she responded. Making such a bold remark in front of her close friends was downright embarrassing.

Fortunately, Katie quickly changed the subject, asking, "Jonah, how do you like Willow Creek so far?"

"It's all right," he said, reaching for the butter. "But the *Ordnung* is different from my home district's. For instance, it seems there are more restrictions here on buggy modifications."

"Anything you need to know about that, you can ask Turner King, my landlord," Tessa suggested. "He and his brothers run a buggy shop, so obviously he's an expert. He's always been very generous to Katie and me as renters, so if you need modifications to your buggy, I'm sure his prices would be reasonable." As soon as the words were out of her mouth, Tessa realized she'd been praising Turner effusively and she wondered if anyone noticed her breathlessness.

To her relief, Jonah asked a question about the use of leaf springs compared with air suspension on the buggies, and all of the men joined the discussion until Katie gave a tiny cough. Tessa knew her sister was politely signaling Mason that they needed to change the conversation to a subject the women could participate in talking about, too.

After supper was over and the dishes put away, everyone said they were too full to eat dessert yet.

"Are you just saying that because you're afraid I burned the lemon squares, too?" Tessa joked.

"I'm sure dessert will be delectable," David said. His flattery felt awkward to Tessa in light of the blatant remarks he'd made about his daughter needing a female influence to help her cook.

"I know!" Faith exclaimed. "Instead of the usual board games, why don't we go outside and play cut the pie?"

"Isn't it still snowing?" David questioned.

"If it is, we won't melt," Faith ribbed, already lacing up her boots.

The group tramped to the flat area at the base of the hill behind the *daadi haus*. The clouds had cleared and the moon lit their path. As they shuffled through the snow, etching a big circle crossed with lines forming eight sections of "pie," Tessa realized it was a good thing there was a fresh layer of snow atop the scant amount beneath it; otherwise someone might have noticed her footprints leading up the hill to Turner's porch. Glancing toward his house, she saw a lamp on. She'd been having so much fun she'd momentarily forgotten how worried she'd been because Turner and Mercy hadn't been home earlier that evening. *I guess everything must be fine*, she thought. *Denki, Lord.*

"Not it!" Hunter suddenly shouted and the rest copied him.

"Looks like you're it, David," Fletcher said when David was silent.

"*Neh*, I'm going to sit this game out," he said, patting his stomach. "I'm too full to move."

Tessa thought if Katie held any hope of her sister and David being a match, she should let it go entirely: Tessa couldn't see herself with a spoilsport.

"I'll keep him company," Anna offered and her husband gave her a knowing nod.

"I'll be it," Jonah gamely volunteered, moving to the middle of the circle as the other players scattered along the lines.

Tessa grinned beneath her scarf. Jonah's personality matched hers more closely than David's did. And although he appeared a year or two younger than she was, he was still closer to her age than David was. *Not that that matters*, she thought. *Turner's nine years older than I am and we get along just fine.* But while she intuitively liked Jonah's character and good humor, for whatever reason she couldn't quite picture him as a suitor.

"No fair!" Katie yelled when Jonah jumped a pie "slice" to tag her. "You can't jump from one piece of pie to another. You have to run within the lines."

"That's not how we play in Ohio," Jonah objected.

"You're not in Ohio any longer," Mason

jested, molding a snowball and lobbing it in Jonah's direction. But Jonah dodged it and it hit Katie instead, disintegrating into a chalky cloud upon impact with her forehead.

"Hey!" Katie indignantly scolded Mason.

"Sorry, I was defending your honor," Mason laughed, just as Faith pitched a snowball at him from behind.

An all-out snowball fight broke out after that, with everyone taking aim at whomever they could hit. The snow was too powdery for anyone to get hurt and, although David stayed on the sidelines, even Anna joined in. When their shouts and squeals became especially loud, Tessa reflexively warned, "We ought to quiet down. We're going to wake the—" but she stopped short of completing her thought.

"The what?" Katie asked. "The only other person nearby is Turner and his lamp is on, so he's not sleeping."

Tessa was at a loss for what to say, but David took advantage of the pause in the snowball fight to interject, "Speaking of people being asleep, I'm almost ready to hit the hay. Are we going to have dessert soon?"

Although the others seemed reluctant to go indoors, Tessa was secretly glad David made the suggestion, and she rewarded him with an especially large lemon square. Not only had he rescued her from Katie's question, but he'd moved the party toward its end. Now that Tessa knew Turner and Mercy were home again, she was eager to find out how they were and where they'd been.

Turner stayed in the shadows on his porch long after he'd watched Tessa and her guests return to the *daadi haus*. He had come out there after putting Mercy to bed because his head ached so severely he felt nauseated and he hoped the fresh air would calm his stomach. But upon realizing Tessa was holding a party, his queasiness worsened.

Rationally, Turner knew he shouldn't be disappointed in her for having fun with her friends. Apparently, that's what people her age did. They nonchalantly accepted rides from *Englischers* and played in the snow with their Amish friends as if they were children. For the second time that day, he felt foolish for ever thinking Tessa might have been interested in his company as a man. He was too old and he had too many responsibilities. Why would she want to spend time with him when she could frolic with her friends?

Their voices traveled clearly across the yard and Turner had tried to discern whether Jeremy was among them, but he couldn't.

From what he could distinguish from their shouting, there was one man in the group who was either visiting or had moved from Ohio. Turner wouldn't be surprised if Katie was trying to match him with Tessa.

Turner felt like a fool for mistaking Tessa's effervescence at the restaurant for genuine happiness to be with him. She'd told him how much she disliked cooking—her conviviality on Thursday was probably mere relief she didn't have to prepare supper that night. Or else she was glad to be with Mercy; the bond between the pair was undeniable. Perhaps she felt she had to humor Turner's suggestions, since technically he was her employer as well as her landlord. As far as Turner knew, maybe she'd accompanied him only out of a sense of duty.

His disenchantment might not have felt so severe if Louisa hadn't just told him the rumor about Jacqueline possibly leaving Willow Creek. The entire evening's events seemed to emphasize Turner's life and responsibilities were in stark contrast to Tessa's. Once again, he reminded himself of the urgent need to concentrate solely on finding his sister. He never should have been distracted by his passing feelings for Tessa in the first place.

Heading back inside, he checked on Mercy and slumped into a chair at the kitchen table. He hadn't eaten, but he wasn't hungry. He bowed his head and prayed for a long while, asking the Lord to move Jacqueline to come home. He lifted his head and then rose to stoke the fire in the wood stove. Upon hearing a knock at the door, he felt his heart gallop with hope: Was God answering his prayers already? But no. It was Tessa, not Jacqueline, who appeared on his doorstep. She was holding a plate wrapped in tinfoil.

"It's *gut* to see you," she said cheerfully. "You weren't here when I stopped by earlier. I was worried."

Turner wasn't about to humiliate himself by telling her about how he'd gone to pick her up, and he couldn't tell her about stopping at the phone shanty, either. "Well, I'm here now," he stated. He didn't intend his words to sound so acerbic, but he offered no further explanation.

Tessa took a step backward, cocking her head. "*Jah*, I can see that. How about Mercy? Is she all right?"

"She's asleep, which is a wonder, considering how much racket you and your guests were making outside."

Tessa's eyes widened. "I'm sorry about that. I tried to keep everyone fairly quiet."

"*Jah*, well, judging from the noise, I'd have guessed you invited *kinner* instead of adults."

"Why is that? Because adults shouldn't have *schpass*?"

Tessa tipped her chin up, as if challenging him to argue, but Turner's head was pounding and he was too tired to quarrel.

"Why have you *kumme* here at this late hour?" he asked directly.

"I thought you might like these lemon squares," she said, "but I see your disposition is sour enough already. *Gut nacht*, Turner."

She whirled around and stormed down the hill. When she slammed the door to the *daadi haus*, he winced at the sound as if he'd been clocked upside his head with a wrench.

Chapter Six

Tessa felt completely humiliated and she couldn't get back inside the *daadi haus* quickly enough. She slapped the plate of lemon squares onto the table. Recalling her mother's adage about the way to a man's heart being through his stomach, she ranted to herself, *That assumes the man actually* has *a heart!*

Not that she wanted to get to Turner King's heart—not anymore, anyway. He was acting like a completely different person than he had on Thursday night, simply because her guests had been a little rowdy. It was as if he was enforcing an ordinance against adults having fun! Tessa doubted they'd made enough noise to wake the baby, but even if they had, she'd apologized for it. If Turner held a grudge for such a small offense, she couldn't imagine how unforgiving he'd be for a substantial one.

His attitude is no different than David's, the old stick-in-the-mud, she thought. How could she have ever entertained romantic notions about Turner? She must have gotten swept up in the drama of his secret about the baby. Or maybe it was that she was so enamored of Mercy she imagined she had developed feelings of affection for Turner, too.

She thought she'd come to understand him a little better over the past couple of weeks and she'd hoped he'd come to understand her better, too. But he obviously didn't, otherwise he wouldn't have acted as if she was prying about where he and Mercy had gone. It wasn't necessarily that Tessa thought she had the right to know, but couldn't Turner at least have given her the courtesy of an explanation? He should have understood her well enough by then to recognize she was worried about what may have happened to Mercy, instead of shutting her out as if she were a snooping pest.

In a way, Tessa was glad Turner had reminded her what he was really like and how he apparently viewed her. It underscored just how much she didn't need a suitor because she didn't want to get married, especially not to such a fuddy-duddy. But he was also a fuddy-duddy who was her employer and landlord as well as a member of her church, and as Tessa prepared for bed she knew she'd have to apologize to him for her flippant remark. But first, she needed to confess her resentment to the Lord. She knelt by the bedside and admitted her transgression, ending her prayer by asking, *Please let my words be acceptable to You and loving toward others.*

When Tessa woke on Sunday morning, her bitterness had melted but she was glad she wouldn't have to see Turner that day. Perhaps all the time she'd spent engaged in his predicament had contributed to her false sense of attraction to him. Although she regretted missing even a single day of seeing Mercy, a little break would do Tessa good. Maybe it would give Turner a new appreciation for her, too.

Tessa joined Katie, Mason and the rest of the large extended Yoder family, including Faith and her husband, Hunter, at the Yoder farmhouse for off-Sunday worship. Afterward, Tessa and Katie helped prepare a light lunch.

"Well?" Katie asked when she and Tessa finally had a moment of privacy as they walked back to Katie's place together while Mason pulled his nephews around the Yoder's yard on a sled. "What did you think?"

"About David, you mean? I think you know what I think."

"Okay, I'll admit he didn't seem like a *gut* match for you. But what about Fletcher's crew member, Jonah?"

"He seemed congenial," she said thoughtfully. "I liked how easygoing he was."

Katie rubbed her gloved hands together in delight. "*Jah*, he was definitely more energetic than David. I think it would be worth it for you to get to know each other better, don't you? Your birthday is coming up on the eighteenth. I could host a party for you and invite him so the two of you could spend more time together."

Tessa had been so consumed with caring for Mercy and protecting Turner's secret, she had forgotten her birthday was drawing near, but she didn't want Katie turning the celebration into another matchmaking opportunity.

"*Denki*, but the truth is I really don't want a suitor, especially not a pretend one. It wouldn't be fair to act as if I'm interested in someone just because I'm afraid *Mamm* would tell me to *kumme* home otherwise," she said as she followed her sister into Katie's house.

"I never suggested you should pretend any-thing—that would be very deceptive," Katie clarified. "But you just said yourself Jonah possesses qualities you like, so why not get to know him better in a casual setting and allow him to get to know you, too? You never know—"

"I said *neh*," Tessa snapped. She'd kept an open mind about meeting David and she'd even entertained the possibility of Turner as a suitor, but look where that had gotten her. This time her position wasn't going to change. "Why can't you understand I really don't want to be courted? Just because you're married doesn't mean I want to be. Not now, anyway."

Katie's eyes welled. "It's not that I want you to get married, Tessa," she said. "At least, not until you want to. It's that I really don't want you to have to leave Willow Creek. I'm trying to think of every possible way to help you stay here."

Tessa felt awful. She hung her cloak on a peg and took her sister by the shoulders. Katie wouldn't look at her as a tear trickled down her cheek. "I'm sorry, Katie. I'm being so de-fensive and self-centered I didn't even think about how my leaving Willow Creek might affect you. I can't even express how much I'd miss you, too. But I'm sure it's not going to happen. In a few weeks, Joseph will need me back again and *Mamm* will never know there was a break in my employment."

"I hope that's true." Katie pushed a tear off her cheek with her palm. "Because I'm going to need you here now more than ever. It's too early to say for sure, but I'm pretty certain I'm with child."

"Katie! That's *wunderbaar* news!" Tessa's joy was immediate and genuine.

"I'm going to the clinic in Highland Springs after school on Wednesday to find out for certain, so I won't be able to have supper with you. Do you suppose we could meet on Friday instead? Say, around five o'clock?"

"*Jah*, whatever works best for you."

"So, about your birthday… Are you at least *open* to the idea of my giving you a party and inviting Jonah?"

Tessa rolled her eyes, but she conceded, "Maybe. We'll see."

"One last thing," Katie added. "If you happen to write home, please don't mention to *Mamm* I'm expecting. I want to tell her in due time."

"Of course I won't," Tessa promised. She and Katie had always shared their deepest secrets with each other before telling anyone else. "But you know *Mamm*—she probably somehow knew about the *bobbel* before you did!"

The two sisters giggled and gave each other a long embrace. But as happy as Tessa was for her sister, an uncomfortable feeling passed over her. It wasn't sadness, exactly. It was more like...like envy. *That's* lecherich, Tessa scolded herself later as she walked home. *Getting married and starting a family is the last thing I want to do right now.* Yet when she opened the door to her empty *daadi haus*, Tessa experienced a sense of loneliness that was so deep she curled up in a ball on her bed and wept until she eventually fell asleep.

Turner was worried about Mercy. She was unusually temperamental and she didn't seem interested in her bottle. He first noticed her mood shortly after he'd finished reading Scripture and praying that morning. She grew increasingly cranky throughout the afternoon and Turner had such a difficult time getting her down for a nap, he ended up holding her the entire time she slept. At first he thought perhaps she'd just become too accustomed to Tessa cuddling her, but when Mercy kept refusing her formula, he became concerned.

He hoped she hadn't caught the stomach flu he'd had.

Now it was evening and as he rocked her in the chair he'd brought down from the attic for Tessa, he studied her face. Even in sleep her bottom lip curled over in a pout and her eyelids were squeezed into two lines curving downward like frowns. Observing her discomfort, Turner felt more anger than forbearance toward his sister for the first time since Jacqueline left Louisa's home. How could she even think about abandoning this vulnerable little child? Having grown up without a mother herself, she ought to have known how important it was for a girl to have a female to nurture and guide her. Some might have argued Jacqueline was only a youngster herself, but Turner figured if she was old enough to give birth to a baby, she was old enough to accept the responsibility for her. After all, he had raised his siblings when he wasn't much older than Jacqueline himself.

But his anger quickly turned back to concern again. What if Jacqueline really did leave town? If Turner hadn't done right in raising her, how would he do right raising her daughter? He couldn't bring Mercy up by himself, nor could he ask Louisa to take the baby, not after all she'd already done and not when her husband was ailing. Turner supposed Rhoda or Ruby would help, but they'd be starting families soon, too. He wasn't confident Mercy would be treated like one of their own children. Turner wanted Mercy to be dearly loved—the way Tessa loved her.

As the thought occurred to him, Turner acknowledged he needed to apologize for the way he'd treated her when she came to visit him. His churlishness had been uncalled for. Yes, Turner's nerves had been frayed because of what Louisa told him, but Tessa had been extraordinarily supportive these past couple of weeks and she deserved better from him.

Deep down, Turner was aware it wasn't merely the news about Jacqueline that had contributed to his boorish behavior toward Tessa. It was also that when he saw her cavorting with her friends in the snow, it shattered his illusion she fancied him the way he was drawn to her. He couldn't blame her for that. He was too burdened with responsibilities, too stodgy and probably too old for someone as vivacious as Tessa. Not that he'd seriously considered the possibility of courtship, exactly, but he had allowed himself to imagine there was a spark of romance between them.

How embarrassing, he thought. *I haven't*

courted for so long I misinterpreted Tessa's attentiveness as attraction. While he couldn't tell Tessa where he'd gone on Saturday because it would mean either admitting he'd intended to pick her up from work or confiding he'd contacted Louisa, he at least could apologize for how he'd behaved when she paid him a visit.

His mind made up, he gently lowered Mercy into her cradle. After praying over her, he crept to his room as quietly as he could. Tending to an upset baby had been more grueling than his most difficult day at the shop and he was beat, but he was still too worried about Mercy to fall asleep. So he pulled a pillow and a quilt into her room and arranged them on the floor, where he eventually drifted into slumber.

Turner was awoken hours later by the sound of what he thought was a coyote yipping and he leaped to his feet, confused about where he was. Then he realized it was Mercy who was howling. Stumbling to the crib in the dark, Turner murmured, "I'm here, Mercy. Your *onkel* is here."

He slid his hand beneath her back and drew her to his chest. Her clothes were damp so he turned on the lamp to change her diaper. Although he hurried through the task as quickly as he could, she cried the whole time. When he lifted her again, his cheek brushed her head. It seemed hot. *She has a fever!* Panicking, Turner wasted no time with a coat—he simply bundled Mercy in the quilt from the floor and charged out of the house down the hill to Tessa's. She'd know what to do.

He was startled to find her waiting with the door open and the kitchen lamp on. Her luxurious hair hung loosely past the blue shawl draped around her shoulders.

"What's wrong, my *schnuck* little *haws*, hmm?" she purred to Mercy and extended her arms to take the baby from Turner.

Turner handed Mercy to her, spouting, "I'm afraid it's the stomach flu. She's been fussy all day and she didn't finish any of her feedings. She has a fever—feel her head. She's hot, isn't she?"

Tessa put her lips to the baby's forehead. Mercy was already quieting, as if she knew she was in good hands again. "She seems a little warm, but I don't think she's actually hot. See how she just rubbed her ear? She might have an earache," Tessa said.

"An earache? She'll need to see a doctor for that, won't she?" Turner asked, but he didn't allow Tessa to answer. "Can it wait until the morning, or should we take her to the emergency room? But if we do that, how will we explain whose *bobbel* she is—*neh, neh,* I don't even care about that. I'll go hitch the horse—"

"Shush!" Tessa demanded, carrying Mercy toward the parlor, lightly jiggling her as she walked. "An earache doesn't necessarily mean an ear infection. Some babies pull at their ears when they're tired. Or she might be teething."

"How can we tell what's wrong with her?"

Instead of answering, Tessa ran her finger along Mercy's bottom gum. "*Jah,* there it is, right there in front. It's a little early, but my sister-in-law's son started teething at three months, too. Or it's possible Mercy is older than I think she is."

"You're sure she doesn't have a fever?" Turner asked. He hoped his question wouldn't offend Tessa but he'd never forgive himself if he neglected to help Mercy while she was under his care.

Tessa pressed her lips to Mercy's forehead a second time before replying thoughtfully, "As I said, she seems a little warm, but not really feverish. Sometimes babies run warm when they're teething. But if it makes you feel better, we can take her temperature. I don't have a baby thermometer, do you?"

"*Neh*, but I could go get one. Some of the *Englisch* convenience stores are open until midnight."

"It's already twelve forty-five," she told him. "But there's a convenience store on the border of Highland Springs that's open twenty-four hours a day. Instead of turning onto the main route, you follow Old County Way all the way until you come to a fork in the road. Bear left and the store is on the right."

In all of his searching for Jacqueline, Turner had never been to the store Tessa described and he wondered how she knew it was open all night. It hardly mattered. "You don't mind staying up with Mercy until I return?"

"Of course not. I've missed her," Tessa said. "But first I'll need you to bring an extra pair of pajamas down from your house. I've got *windle* but I'll need more formula and spare bottles. It probably makes sense for us to keep her supplies at both houses anyway, instead of carting them back and forth."

Shooting out the door and up the hill to his house, Turner gathered the items Tessa required and sprinted back to the *daadi haus*. When he returned, Tessa was swaying in half twists with the baby in her arms. Mercy's cries had stopped completely and she was gripping a lock of Tessa's hair.

"I think you're going to have to untangle me," Tessa told Turner. "She won't let go."

Turner spoke in a soothing voice. "*Neh, neh*, Mercy. Don't pull. We mustn't hurt Tessa."

His hands trembled as he gingerly pried Mercy's fingers, one by one, from Tessa's tresses. He was close enough to smell Tessa's shampoo, and whether it was the fragrance, the nearness to her or his anxiety about the baby, he felt heady with nervousness.

Once he freed Tessa's hair from Mercy's clutches, Turner uttered, "I'll be back soon," in a husky voice and started toward the door.

"Turner, wait," Tessa said, stopping him midstride. "I'm confident Mercy will be fine—she seems more comfortable already. Getting a thermometer is only a precaution for your sake, so there's no need to rush. You must slow down or you'll have an accident. Go put on your coat and hat, and don't forget to take money with you or you'll end up making the trip twice."

As he turned and faced her, Turner ruefully thought she had never appeared as lovely to him as she did in that moment. It wasn't her glossy hair, chocolate-colored eyes or flawless complexion that made her so: it was her gracious care about him, despite his cloddish behavior toward her. He felt like falling to his knees to ask her forgiveness, but there would be time for that later.

"*Denki* for the reminders," he said. "You always seem to think of everything."

Tessa's directions led him straight to the convenience store. It wasn't surprising he'd never visited this particular shop; it wasn't one of the chain stores he usually frequented and from the outside it looked deserted. Inside, he discovered it wasn't as well kept as the other stores and he searched the dusty aisles hoping to spot the kind of baby thermometer Mercy needed.

"You need help finding something?" a young *Englisch* woman asked. She wore heavy eye makeup and ripped jeans, and her left nostril was pierced with three silver hoops.

"I'm looking for a baby thermometer," Turner said.

"Oh, yeah, they should be right over here," the woman replied, leading him to an assortment of gauze, aspirin and antiseptics. She scanned the items hanging from small metal rods, but didn't find what he was looking for. "Zander," she called to a blond guy wearing a sweatshirt monogrammed with the letters of a local college. "Do we have any baby thermometers?"

Please, Gott, *let them be in stock*, Turner prayed.

"Try the next aisle over, the one by the diapers," he shouted from his perch behind the cash register. "Jackie was shelving inventory. She probably messed up again."

"Yep, here it is," the girl said, holding a box up victoriously. "Somebody needs to train that girl better."

Zander snickered. "Not gonna happen. Artie canned her on Saturday. She barely made it through the trial period."

"Oh, that's too bad," the girl replied, bringing Turner's purchase to the counter for him. "I really liked Jacqueline. She was sweet."

Jacqueline? Turner felt as if his legs were made of rubber. His hand shook as he reached to give Zander a twenty-dollar bill. "Is Jacqueline Amish by any chance?" he asked casually.

Zander's laugh exposed white, perfectly aligned teeth. "She didn't dress like it, but that would explain a lot if she was. Like why she always asked me to ring up the magazines and booze."

Turner steadied himself against the check-out counter. "Do you know where she lives?"

Zander squinted at Turner suspiciously. "Why? Is she your wife? Kind of young for you, but I guess that's the Amish way, huh?"

Turner held his tongue. If he weren't so desperate to find Jacqueline, he would never disclose his personal situation to a stranger, especially not to an *Englischer* with a foul mouth. "I think she might be my sister." He repeated, "Do you know where she lives?"

"Never asked." Zander handed Turner his change, pushed the plastic bag containing the thermometer across the counter and said dismissively, "Have a good night."

But Turner wasn't going to be dissuaded so easily. "Listen, my sister is… She's missing and I think the girl who worked here might be her. Did she have long dark hair and blue eyes?"

"Nope, this Jacqueline is a blonde," Zander said. "With green eyes. There's no way she's your sister."

The young woman tipped her head. "Why are you telling him she—"

Zander cut her off. "You'd better go reshelve Jackie's mistakes, Chloe. Artie won't be pleased if he finds out you've been standing around yapping instead of working."

Chloe opened her mouth but then closed it again and disappeared into the back room. Turner got the sense she was about to tell him something about the girl who worked there, but he couldn't very well follow her. Besides, he needed to get back to Mercy. Deciding he'd return the next day to talk to the staff again, he exited the store.

He wasn't halfway across the parking lot when a female called to him.

"Hey, mister!" Chloe was carrying a big plastic bag of garbage. "Listen, I've got to be quick or Zander will come looking for me. That girl, Jackie. She does too have dark hair and blue eyes."

Turner knew it! Denki, *Lord*, he immediately prayed, his hopes burgeoning. But why did Zander lie about what Jacqueline looked like?

Chloe continued speaking as they walked toward the dumpster. "I don't know where she lives, but our manager, Artie, might. He usually shows up between five thirty and six each night. But the thing is, well, he's paying some of us under the table, 'cause we're minors. Not everyone has a valid work permit, if you know what I mean."

Turner understood. "So he might not be willing to tell me anything about her?"

"Right." Chloe hurled the bag over the side of the dumpster and wiped her hands on her jeans. "I know Amish people don't usually do this kind of thing, but you could mention the licensing authorities. I mean, please don't really report him—if he gets into trouble I could lose my job and I really need the money. But you know, you could drop some hints."

He smiled widely. This young girl with thick makeup and tattered clothing was going out of her way, even risking her job, to help him. Would he have done the same for her or for any other young *Englischer*? His attitude had to change.

"Denki," he said and added the blessing, *"Gott segen eich*, Chloe."

"Your sister's a good kid. I hope you find her." She scrambled back to the store.

I do, too, Turner thought. *I do, too.*

After easing Mercy's pain by placing a cold cloth on her gums, Tessa was able to prompt her to take a bottle. After she burped a couple of times, the baby seemed content to cuddle, taking in Tessa's face with her big, innocent eyes.

"You feel better now, don't you, Mercy?" Tessa murmured. "I feel better, too, now that you're in my arms again. Two days away from you is two days too many."

"Ah-ah-ah." The baby seemed to agree.

"But I'm not so sure our friend, Turner, feels better. And he probably won't until he takes your temperature and is assured you don't have a fever, but that's just because he cares about you so much."

Tessa continued talking to Mercy until the baby's eyelids closed. Sitting on the sofa in the dim light, she listened to Mercy's rhythmic breathing and thought about Turner. She had never seen him so alarmed. Rather, she hadn't seen him so alarmed since the night Mercy arrived on the doorstep. He'd worn the same aghast, defenseless expression tonight as he'd worn then. Once again, her gall over his curt behavior was superseded by deep sympathy for his situation.

She couldn't help but wonder if Lynne knew what a burden she'd placed on Turner by leaving the baby in his care. Yes, Tessa was there to help, but Lynne wouldn't have known that. On the contrary, by requesting Turner not tell anyone about Mercy, Lynne essentially ensured the burden would fall entirely on him. Lynne undoubtedly knew he'd accept the responsibility with unflinching commitment, but Tessa could see it was taking a toll on him. Whoever Lynne was, Turner must have cared about her deeply to make such a sacrifice. And it was clear he cared about Mercy every bit as much. *Despite his sullenness, his devotion is admirable*, Tessa mused.

Then she admitted to herself it wasn't merely admirable—it was attractive. Turner's commitment to those he loved was more appealing to Tessa than a sense of levity in someone like Jonah could ever be. Which wasn't to say she didn't appreciate a sense of fun in a man, but that she was surprised by how drawn she was to Turner, in spite of his serious nature.

It hardly matters, she thought. *He's obviously preoccupied with bigger concerns. And even if he was interested in courting someone, he's made it clear he thinks I'm too... What was it he called me? Young and carefree.* What would it take for him to see that, while she might be cheery and social, she was also thoughtful and responsible?

Tessa was so deep in thought she didn't hear Turner's quiet arrival some time later. His pallor was no longer as white as milk and he projected renewed energy when he presented Tessa with the sterile thermometer.

Taking it from him, she said, "While I'm

doing this, why don't you fix us a cup of tea? I think we could both use a little refreshment."

Turner followed her suggestion and when he returned with the cups several minutes later, Tessa grinned. "99.2," she announced. "That's completely normal for a baby her age."

"*Denki*, Lord!" Turner yawped, nearly spilling their hot beverages. "And *denki*, Tessa. What would I have done without you? I don't know how I'll ever repay you."

"As I told you from the start, I *want* to help," Tessa emphasized, hoping Turner would hear the sincerity in her tone and understand she was speaking as a friend, not merely as a hired nanny. "You're not indebted. You don't owe me a thing."

"Actually, I do. I owe you an apology." Turner sat on a chair across from Tessa, took a sip of tea and then set his cup aside and cleared his throat. His eyes were the color of thunderclouds. "I'm sorry about how I treated you last night. You must have been appalled by my rudeness—I know I am."

Hearing Turner openly admit his shortcoming filled Tessa with warmth. She met his gaze and said, "I forgive you. And I'm sorry I made an insulting comment about your disposition. I was hurt by your attitude, but my remark was very immature."

"It was also accurate. I can be a real killjoy sometimes," Turner confessed. He picked up his teacup and stared into it. "You and your guests weren't making too much noise at all. I think maybe I was envious."

"Envious? But why?"

"Because you all were having *schpass* and I was... Well, I wasn't."

"That's understandable. You've had a lot on your mind lately."

Turner shook his head. "You have no idea."

Tessa realized he might think she was being nosy, but she had to ask, "Do you want to tell me about it?"

Tessa's voice was so sympathetic and her presence so reassuring Turner took a deep breath. He knew his sister wouldn't want him to tell Tessa that Jacqueline was Mercy's mother, but this was no longer about what Jacqueline wanted. It was about what Turner *needed*. And what he needed was encouragement and support from someone he trusted. From Tessa. He sighed and then his words rushed forth like the creek's current in springtime. He confided everything, beginning with his parents' death to the time

Jacqueline moved to Louisa's home in Ohio and straight through to his conversation with Chloe at the convenience store. Twice in the telling he had to stop and blink back tears, but Tessa's mild expression never changed. Her eyes reflected kindness and sensitivity. She softly patted Mercy on the back, but other than that, she didn't move an inch. When Turner finally finished sharing his burden, he simultaneously felt fifty pounds lighter yet completely wrung out.

To his grateful relief, Tessa didn't speak a word of criticism against Jacqueline, she didn't give him unsolicited advice and she didn't ask him any questions, save one: "What can I do to help you find your sister?"

"You're already doing it," Turner said. He paused before adding, "If possible, I'd like to talk to Artie right when he gets to the store in the afternoon. Chloe said he usually arrives between five thirty and six. I'm not sure when I'll be back. I suppose it depends on if I find out where Jacqueline is living and whether she's home when I get there. Do you think you could—"

"I'll watch Mercy for as long as you need me to," Tessa offered. "So please take your time. And as for the rest of tonight, I think

Mercy should stay here since I know how to treat her gums."

"She's not going to let you get any sleep."

"We'll be fine. I'm more concerned about *you* getting sleep. You should go home and get to bed. You need to rest so you can think clearly."

"All right," Turner agreed reluctantly.

"I'll be praying for you about your conversation with Artie," Tessa said as she walked him to the door where they both paused at the same time. They were standing so close he could hear Mercy breathing.

"*Denki*, I appreciate that. And I'm so grateful you knew how to ease Mercy's discomfort." Turner put his hand on the doorknob. Before twisting it, he asked, "By the way, how is it you were still awake when we showed up?" he asked.

"Sunday is visiting day, so the last of my unruly guests had just left and I was cleaning up after them," Tessa said with a wink.

A grin curled Turner's mouth for the first time all night.

Then Tessa said in a more serious tone, "To be honest, I wasn't actually awake until I heard Mercy crying."

Turner was incredulous. "You heard her from all the way up at my house?"

Tessa shrugged. "Either that, or I heard her as you were running down the hill. All I remember is I was startled awake and I knew right away Mercy needed my help."

"Really?" He was impressed. "I guess that's what they call maternal instinct," he said.

"Maternal instinct?" Tessa repeated, wrinkling her forehead. Then a smile sparkled across her face. "*Jah*, I suppose that's exactly what it was."

Turner wasn't sure what he'd said to make her appear so pleased, but whatever it was, he hoped he'd say something like it again very soon.

Chapter Seven

Tessa returned to the parlor and ruminated over Turner's disclosure. Suddenly, everything made sense: his guarded exterior, the trips Katie and Tessa saw him making, Mercy's resemblance to him. What was especially clear was why he seemed so intolerant of *Englischers*. Tessa regretted making unfavorable assumptions about his character, but at least those thoughts had been fleeting—she felt worse for holding a longstanding opinion he was fundamentally sullen. It was no wonder he was slow to smile; his burdens were greater than any she had ever carried.

As troubled as she was about Turner's heartaches, Tessa simultaneously felt honored he'd confided in her about them. He didn't have a choice when it came to telling her about Mercy, since she knew about the baby even before he did. But telling her about Jacqueline was of his own accord. Surely this meant he trusted her deeply? Now more than ever Tessa intended to show him how worthy she was of his confidence.

Sighing, Mercy scrunched her face in her sleep. Over the course of a short time Mercy had grown noticeably, becoming even chubbier if that was possible. Tessa's muscles ached from holding her, but she was reluctant to put the baby down. It occurred to her if Turner was able to locate Jacqueline and convince her to come home with him, Tessa no longer would be taking care of Mercy. She hadn't realized how attached she'd grown to her until she had to face the imminence of letting her go. Tears streamed from her eyes and she tried to wipe them away with the corner of her apron, but they came too fast. She cried noiselessly so as not to wake Mercy.

I must be overly tired, she told herself. But she knew that wasn't what was wrong, not entirely. The fact was she'd come to treasure her relationship with Turner as much as she cherished her bond with Mercy. They'd become a family of sorts and she didn't want their time together to end, just as she previously hadn't wanted her days living alone to end. *How did that happen?* she lamented.

How did I change from wishing I could stay single indefinitely to yearning for a husband and bobbel? She knew the answer to her own question: Turner and Mercy were what happened. As a tear rolled from her cheek and dribbled onto Mercy's forehead, Tessa realized if she didn't go to bed now, her sobs would get the best of her and she'd wind up waking the baby.

Since she was too tired to take out the big drawer she used as a crib for Mercy, Tessa arranged a place on her own bed where she could safely lay the baby for the night. Before she settled next to her, Tessa pulled her prayer *kapp* from the bedpost and knelt beside the bed. She thanked God for easing Mercy's discomfort and asked Him to help Turner find Jacqueline and to know what to say when he did. She ended by saying, *Lord, I understand it's best for* mamm *and* bobbel *to be reunited, but it hurts to let go of Mercy, so please give me Your peace.*

In the morning Tessa woke to Mercy making gurgling sounds next to her. She reached over and placed her hand on the baby's belly. "I'm glad to hear your teeth aren't bothering you this morning," she said. "Is there any chance you'd let me sleep a few more minutes?"

Every time Tessa closed her eyes and fell

silent, Mercy animatedly waved her arms and made lip-smacking noises Tessa recognized meant she was hungry, so Tessa picked her up and ambled into the kitchen. As coffee percolated on the stove top, she cracked two eggs into a pan and then prepared Mercy's formula so they could leisurely eat their breakfast together.

"Look, Mercy," Tessa said later that morning as she pulled construction paper from a drawer. "I've been making Valentine's Day cards. Maybe when you take a nap this afternoon, I'll make more. I might even make one for your *onkel*."

But just after Tessa put Mercy down for her late afternoon nap, Turner arrived. "I didn't stop by this morning because I thought you girls might need your sleep," he said. "I wanted to see how Mercy is and ask if there's anything you need before I head to Highland Springs."

"She's sleeping soundly after a very active day. You'd never know she was in pain from teething, although it's bound to come and go."

"It was probably just a ploy to visit you last night," Turner joked.

"She doesn't need a ploy—she's *wilkom* any time."

"Does that go for me, too?" Turner asked.

Tessa couldn't tell if he was earnestly uncertain or if he was being flirtatious. Erring on the side of caution, she said, "Of course that goes for you, too."

"In that case, I'll stay for a visit after I return from Highland Springs." There was a hint of apprehension in Turner's voice. Tessa understood: she was probably as nervous about what he might discover as he was. She didn't know if he could bear the dejection if he learned Jacqueline had already left the area.

"I'll be waiting," she said. "I'll even make supper."

"I might not be back until late."

"That's okay, it will keep," Tessa said. Then, to encourage him, she added, "I'll make plenty, in case your sister is hungry, too."

This time Turner's voice sounded optimistic when he replied, "*Denki*. We'll look forward to that."

Turner had possessed an abundant amount of nervous energy all day. With his brothers away, he had hoped to use the quietude to concentrate on reconciling the bookkeeping, a project he kept procrastinating, but he was too wound up. Since there were no repairs scheduled he had poured himself into filling their next wheel order. But now, as he headed toward the convenience store, he suddenly felt depleted, as if he could hardly lift his horse's reins.

To distract himself from the whorls of dread twisting in his stomach, he reflected on Tessa's hopefulness he'd find his sister. *This must be how Patrick and Mark feel to have the faithful reassurance of their wives. Whoever Tessa chooses to marry will be a very blessed man.*

Even as the idea crossed his mind, Turner felt a stab of sorrow, knowing *he* could never be that man. Yes, Tessa knew his deepest secret yet seemingly held no judgment against Jacqueline or him. But knowing what happened in someone else's family and having it happen in one's own family were two different matters. Even if his farfetched dream came true and Tessa was willing to accept him as her suitor, Turner could never marry her, so courting her was futile.

Considering what happened as a result of him raising his sister, Turner was absolutely panicked at the possibility he might have to raise his niece. He'd do it, if it came to that, because he loved her and because he had no other choice, just as he'd had no other choice but to raise Jacqueline. But he could choose whether or not to raise a daughter, because he could choose not to marry and thus spare a potential wife from the kind of affliction he was experiencing now.

Turner shook his head and reminded himself he had to stay focused on the task at hand. He thought about what he was going to say to Jacqueline when he found her. He'd tell her he loved her, of course, and that she always had a home—she and Mercy both—as well as a family who wanted to help her. He'd urge her to return, letting her know that although she might wish she hadn't made certain choices in her life so far, she could make better decisions now. He'd say he thought she'd regret leaving the Amish, but she'd never regret anything as much as she'd regret leaving Mercy. And he would remind her that although she might turn her back on the Lord, God would pursue her with His unfailing love.

Although he arrived at his destination later than he intended, Turner took the time to pause before entering the convenience store, asking the Lord to help him demonstrate grace and patience to the *Englisch*.

"Artie?" Turner questioned when he approached an overweight, middle-aged man with a moustache and thick-rimmed glasses standing behind the checkout counter.

"Who's asking?" The man was obviously surveying Turner's clothes and hat.

Turner swallowed, knowing if he wanted information from the man, he'd have to be forthcoming. "My name is Turner King. I believe you know my sister, Jacqueline."

Artie stopped counting the bills he was holding long enough to cock his head and say, "Jacqueline? Can't say I've met anyone by that name."

"You might know her as Jackie. Or Lynne," Turner said, realizing Zander probably warned Artie about their early morning conversation, and the manager might feel threatened by Turner's presence. "I'd just like to speak with my sister."

"Sorry. Wish I could help." Artie wrapped an elastic band around the wad of bills before pocketing them.

Turner felt desperate. *Lord, please guide me.* "I think you can," he persisted. "If you tell me where she lives, I'd appreciate it."

Artie squared his shoulders. "She didn't mention where she lives."

Turner pointed out Artie's slip of the tongue. "Then you admit she *did* work here! She must have given you her address when she filled out an application."

"My filing system is a mess," Artie claimed.

Suddenly, it dawned on Turner that anyone who paid his employees under the table wouldn't have made them fill out legitimate applications. "Someone here must have seen her arriving at or leaving work. Was she within walking distance, or did she get a ride in a car?"

Artie lumbered out from behind the counter. He was even taller than Turner and twice his width. He pointed to a No Loitering sign hanging on the wall. "I've told you I don't know anything about the girl, so unless you're going to buy something, it's time for you to leave."

Averse as he was to contacting the *Englisch* authorities, Turner recalled Chloe's advice and said, "She's a minor and she's missing, so if I can't find her myself, I'll have to visit the police. Perhaps by then you'll have found her address, and you can tell them when they question you and your staff about her employment here."

"Ha," Artie scoffed, but he dropped his shoulders. "The Amish don't get involved with the police."

"Not as a rule, no," Turner said, heading for

the door. "But we do when conscience dictates or we have no other recourse."

"Hold on." Artie's tone was urgent. "Payday starts tomorrow night at six and it ends the second I walk out that door at seven fifteen. The kids know there are no substitutions, no excuses, no exceptions. I pay in cash so they need to come in and pick it up in person. If your sister was working here—and I'm not admitting she was—that's her one chance to collect her wages. And if she doesn't, you might try asking Skylar when he comes in for his pay. Muscular guy, curly hair like a lion's. You'll recognize him because he wears cargo shorts, even in winter. But I'm warning you—no drama in front of my employees or customers."

"You have my word I won't cause any trouble," Turner said emphatically, extending his hand to shake Artie's the way the *Englisch* did. "*Denki*, sir. You've been very helpful."

It was only a little after six o'clock when Tessa heard a knock. Surprised Turner was back already, she wiped her hands on her apron. She alternately had been fearing and looking forward to this moment. If Turner hadn't found Jacqueline, he'd likely be overcome with sorrow. If he had found her and convinced her to come back with him, he'd be elated. That was exactly what Tessa wanted, but it would also mean her responsibility to care for Mercy had come to an end. She smoothed her hair and tried to relax her posture before tugging the door open.

"Hello, Tessa." It was Melinda Schrock. "I hope I didn't catch you in the middle of eating supper?"

Because Mercy was wide awake and gumming a cold cloth in the parlor, Tessa stepped outside onto the porch, pulling the doorknob close to her back. "Actually, I am in the middle of making it," she said honestly, hoping Melinda would take the hint and keep their conversation short. "What can I do for you, Melinda?"

"It's more like what I can do for you," Melinda boasted. "I'm here to offer you my shift tomorrow at Schrock's."

"What? Why?" Tessa stalled, trying to come up with a truthful reason she couldn't work the following day.

"I have the opportunity to visit Jesse's relatives in your hometown, Shady Valley, tonight and tomorrow," she said. "His brother was in town for business today and he invited us to a party for his wife. Sort of short notice, but Joseph said he didn't mind, as long as you fill in for me."

Tessa hugged her torso to keep warm. Without knowing whether Turner had located Jacqueline, she couldn't risk not being available to watch Mercy. "I'm sorry, but I can't."

"Why not?" Melinda asked. "I thought you'd jump at the chance to earn a full day's pay."

"Ordinarily, I would. *Denki* for thinking of me," Tessa said in a sweet tone so Melinda wouldn't be too angry. "But not this time."

"Why not?" Melinda demanded.

Tessa knew from experience Melinda didn't take the word *no* easily. "I have a… family matter to take care of this week," she said. Perhaps it wasn't *her* family matter, but it was the closest reason to the truth she could offer.

"What kind of family matter?"

Tessa worried she was running out of time before Mercy began crying. "It's private, so I'd rather not discuss it. I'm sorry you'll miss your trip. At least it wasn't something you were anticipating for a long time, so I hope you'll get over your disappointment quickly."

Melinda's eyes widened. It was clear she was curious but since Tessa had put her foot down firmly and Melinda probably understood she couldn't get more information out of her, she resorted to cajoling. "Joseph's the one who will be disappointed. He always talks about how willing you are to help. Wait until he finds out you turned down the chance to work for an entire day without even really giving a reason. He's going to feel slighted."

Tessa recognized Melinda was only trying to manipulate her, but her comments hit a nerve anyway. What if Joseph really was offended Tessa didn't fill in for her? And what if he decided he didn't want Tessa to come back to her job when business increased? The efforts she'd made to stay in Willow Creek would be for nothing—she'd end up back in Shady Valley after all. *But Joseph would never fire me over something like that. Would he?* she wondered. Right then she resolved to pray that wouldn't happen but to accept it if it did. It would break her heart, but she'd rather lose her job and have to return home than to let Turner down when he was this close to finding Jacqueline. Tessa's commitment to him—and to Mercy—was more important than her own plans and desires.

"That's not my intention at all and I'd feel terrible if he was offended," Tessa finally replied. "But Joseph understands about family commitments, so I think it's unlikely he'll feel put out. If anything, I'd think he'd feel slighted by you, since he gave you the privilege of working full time instead of me, and now you'd rather go to a party than honor your work commitment."

Melinda looked dumbfounded and Tessa took advantage of her silence to say, "As I mentioned, I'm cooking supper, so I need to say *gut nacht* now, Melinda."

She could hear Melinda stomping down the stairs like a child throwing a tantrum, so when heavy footfalls sounded on the porch a few minutes later, she assumed her coworker had returned to badger her again.

"I'm sorry, but the answer is still *neh*," she said as she swung the door open.

"What was the question?" Turner asked. He was standing alone but he was grinning—a good sign.

"*Ach!* Turner, *kumme* in," she prattled. "You look pleased. Did you find Jacqueline?"

"Not yet, but I'm getting closer," he announced, wiping his feet.

"That's *wunderbaar* news!" Without thinking, she reached out and squeezed his arm for emphasis. In response, he placed his hand over hers and gently squeezed back.

"*Jah*, it is," he agreed exuberantly.

Sensing everything was about to change,

Tessa memorized the way she felt with Turner's large calloused hand enveloping hers while the baby cooed happily in the next room. When she could preserve the moment no longer she pulled away, saying, "How about if you go get Mercy while I put supper on the table? Then you can tell me all about your trip."

Whether it was from what he'd just discovered concerning Jacqueline or from the silkiness of Tessa's fingers beneath his, Turner felt lighter than he had in years. It was as if all the tension he ever carried in his head, jaw and neck had metamorphosed into a fluttering hopefulness, and he was bursting at the seams to share his exciting news with Tessa.

She insisted on holding Mercy so he could eat, and he dug into his plate of shepherd's pie with gusto. In between bites, he recounted his interaction with Artie, ending by telling Tessa how confident he was he'd see Jacqueline the next day.

"I'm sure she's in need of money, so she'll be there," he said, helping himself to a second serving of pie.

Tessa placed her prayer *kapp* strings over her shoulder so Mercy couldn't yank them as she fed the baby her bottle. "Your *mamm* is going to be surprised at how pudgy you are now, little *haws*," she said to the baby.

"That's provided I can persuade her to *kumme* home," Turner said. When Tessa squinted, biting her lip, he asked, "What's wrong? You look doubtful."

"I have no doubt you'll find Jacqueline. But is talking to her the most effective way to persuade her to return?"

Turner was baffled. "What do you suggest? I can't *insist* she return and I'm not going to call the authorities."

"Of course not. But have you considered bringing Mercy with you?" Tessa asked. "My intuition tells me it was excruciating for her to leave this little *bobbel* the first time, and as soon as she sees her *dochder* she'll never want to part with her again."

"Aha. And since Jacqueline doesn't have a job to support a baby, much less to support herself, she'll be more than willing to return home." Turner marveled at the wisdom of Tessa's suggestion. "That's a terrific idea."

Tessa moved the baby to her knee and tapped her back until Mercy released a most unladylike belch. Turner and Tessa both chuckled.

"There is a favor I'd like to ask," Turner said. "Would you be willing to *kumme* with us?"

Tessa didn't hesitate. "Sure. I'd be happy to keep Mercy calm during the trip."

"It's not just Mercy you keep calm—I feel more tranquil in your presence, too."

A smile dawned across Tessa's features. Turner was pleased she seemed to accept his compliment. "Please pass the salt," she said as she scooped shepherd's pie onto her plate.

"Salt?" he taunted, holding the shaker just beyond her reach. "This meal is perfectly seasoned. Why do you need salt?"

"Perfectly seasoned? You should tell my *mamm* that," Tessa replied, tugging the salt shaker from his fingers. "She doesn't exactly consider me to be a very *gut* cook."

"Really? I knew you didn't *like* to cook, but there's no question in my mind you *can* cook. Your meals prove otherwise."

"*Denki*, but only a bachelor could say that about my meals," Tessa teased. "According to my *mamm*, the reason I'm not being courted and haven't gotten married yet is because of my culinary skills. 'The way to a man's heart is through his stomach,' she always says."

"I hardly think your cooking is the reason you aren't married yet," Turner said.

"*Neh?*" Tessa asked coyly. She paused to lick gravy from her fork. "So what you're saying is there are far more obvious reasons a man wouldn't want to court or marry me?"

"*Neh, neh,* I didn't mean it that way!" Turner protested. "I only meant the meal is very *gut.*"

Tessa's eyes met his. "I'm glad you like it."

"I like you very much." Chagrined, Turner immediately corrected himself. "It. I like *it* very much."

To distract Tessa from his blunder, he quickly changed the subject. "So, are you going to tell me what you meant by what you said when you answered the door tonight?"

When Tessa was done explaining about how Melinda asked her to cover her shift at the shop, Turner said, "*Ach!* As much as I appreciate you turning down a shift to watch Mercy, in the future please do what's best for you. If you wanted to work tomorrow, I would have found a way to watch Mercy. That's one of the advantages of being a business owner—especially a business owner whose brothers recently took time off from work. They owe me extra hours at the shop."

"But what excuse would you have given them?" Tessa asked.

"It would have taken a little creativity, but I would have worked it out."

"Speaking of working it out," Tessa began,

"Katie can't meet me for supper on Wednesday evening, so she wants to meet me on Friday night instead. I already told her *jah*, but now that we're so close to finding—"

"Don't be *lecherich*. There's no need to cancel on Katie. Who knows? By Friday evening, we both might be eating supper with our sisters!"

"*Gott* willing," Tessa said.

But the following evening, after arriving early, parking at a gravelly rest area across the street from the convenience store and waiting for what felt like days, they still hadn't spotted Jacqueline. Instead, they witnessed a handful of adults who appeared to be customers going into and out of the store, as well as several youth, including Chloe, who entered and exited a couple of minutes later with their hands shoved into their pockets or clutching their purses. Meanwhile, Mercy's fussing erupted into a full-scale lamentation. It seemed the more her volume increased, the more Turner's hopes decreased.

"I need to stretch," he said and leaped down from the buggy. Treading back and forth along the shoulder of the road, he trained his eye on the door to the convenience store. Turner didn't wear a watch, but he figured it was at least seven, maybe later. Hadn't Artie said the employees needed to collect their pay by seven fifteen, no exceptions?

Right when he was about to rejoin Tessa in the buggy, Turner noticed a silver car pulling into the lot. It parked halfway between the buggy and the mini-mart and it was angled in such a way it partially obscured Turner's view of the store's entrance. Since the driver got out on the other side of the car to enter the shop, Turner couldn't get a good look except to notice it was a male. *Why hasn't Jacqueline* kumme *yet?* he wondered, shaking his head.

A moment later, a large man exited. Turner would have recognized Artie's shape anywhere. The manager plodded to a sports car, squeezed into the front seat and drove away. Recalling Artie's rule that payday was over once he left the premises, Turner's hopes were completely dashed.

"Turner!" Katie stepped down from the buggy, clutching Mercy. "Look! Isn't that the kind of car the person who dropped off Mercy was driving? I'm almost sure—"

Turner didn't wait for her to finish. He raced across the lot and reached the vehicle at the same time a curly-haired young man wearing shorts came out of the store.

"Skylar!" Turner shouted, stepping in between the man and his car. "I need to talk to you about my sister, Jacqueline."

"Sure, no problem," the man replied, but they were interrupted by the sound of the baby's diminished cries and Tessa's approaching footsteps. "Is that Mercy I hear?"

So Tessa was right: Skylar *was* there the night Mercy was dropped off. Or at least his car had been. Turner nearly committed the sin of physically harming another person when he gripped the young man by his shoulders, spinning him so they were eye to eye. "What do you know about my sister's baby?"

"Turner," Tessa cut in. A car had driven up and its high beams illuminated the two men.

Turner released his hold on Skylar. "Why don't we walk over to my buggy to talk?"

"That's a good idea. Let me ask my wife to join us," Skylar said. Until that moment, Turner hadn't realized a woman was sitting in the passenger's seat. Opening the door, Skylar bent down and said, "Charlotte, these folks want to talk to us about Jackie and Mercy."

The woman emerged from the car and she and Skylar glanced over their shoulders at the convenience store before accompanying Turner and Tessa to the buggy, where Charlotte and Tessa facilitated an awkward round of introductions.

"What do you know about my sister's baby?" Turner repeated impatiently. "Did you leave Mercy on my doorstep or do you know who did?"

"I understand the situation is upsetting, but if you give me a moment, I'll tell you everything I know," Skylar promised. He explained how he and Charlotte led a kind of underground ministry for runaway teenagers. Skylar worked at Artie's because he believed the best way to help kids in trouble was to build relationships with them. Since Artie mostly employed minors who didn't have work permits, the store was an ideal place to reach youth who needed help, although Skylar had to be careful Artie didn't find out about their ministry.

Turner was skeptical. "You have a ministry for Amish runaways?"

"For *any* underage runaways," Charlotte answered. "We primarily help *Englisch* kids, but you'd be surprised how many Amish teens we come into contact with, too."

Turner *was* surprised to hear that, but his urgent concern was finding out more about Jacqueline, not about their ministry. He pushed them to answer his questions.

"We don't know where she lives—she was extremely guarded about it," Skylar told him.

"Charlotte and I left Mercy with you at Jackie's request. She was conflicted about whether she was going to return home or try to start over in Philadelphia."

Turner's blood was boiling. "You said you *help* runaways. How is separating a *mamm* from her *bobbel* and her family helpful? What gives you the right to—"

Tessa cleared her throat, which Turner recognized as a reminder to keep his temper in check. He let his sentence drop.

"You've misunderstood, Turner," Charlotte said softly. "We weren't trying to *separate* Jackie and Mercy. We were trying to keep them together. Jackie was… She was in a bad way. Whether it was reasonable or not, her biggest fear was social services might take the baby from her. We asked if anyone in her family could care for Mercy until she was thinking straight again. Meanwhile, she had to get a job to support herself."

"Our hope for her was that she'd reunite with her family and her Amish community," Skylar asserted. "Unlike some of the kids we meet who suffer abuse at home or who are struggling with addiction—and worse—we knew Jackie comes from a stable, loving family. It seemed the only thing keeping her from returning home was her sense of shame."

"We spoke with her about the forgiveness we have in Christ," Charlotte said. "And she told us she'd repented and asked for God's forgiveness, but she was having a difficult time forgiving herself."

Skylar concluded, "She seemed to miss her family and community a lot. So when Artie fired her, we thought for sure she'd finally return home."

"She didn't," Turner stated flatly, his voice hoarse. He was so deflated he feared he might cry in front of everyone.

"It's possible she'll show up for one of our Sunday night dinners again. If not, we'll continue to keep our eyes peeled for her," Charlotte offered. "We have contacts throughout the state, so if we find out she's left the area, we can enlist their help, too."

"Yeah, we'll definitely do that, but my guess is without her final pay she probably can't afford a bus ticket," Skylar reasoned. "So she won't go far. Not unless she borrows money from someone."

Turner was willing to clutch at any straw of hope. "That might be true…"

"On the off chance she does borrow cash or had any savings, you might want to stake out the bus depot," Skylar suggested, pulling out a cell phone. He tapped the keyboard before lifting the phone to his ear. "What time does the bus run to Philadelphia from Highland Springs?" he asked. "Monday, Wednesday and Friday nights at seven thirty-eight? Okay, thanks."

Turner blew air through his lips. Zander said she was fired on Saturday, so the first bus she could have caught left on Monday evening. They might have missed her by a day.

Tessa immediately offered consolation. "I think Skylar's right—she probably doesn't have the means to leave. But just in case, there's another bus running tomorrow night. We can watch for her on that one."

Turner massaged his neck. It seemed he was no closer to finding Jacqueline now than he'd been when she first left Louisa's, and he was exhausted.

"Why don't we head back to Willow Creek, Turner? We can check the phone shanty for messages on the way," Tessa coaxed.

"All right," he agreed. Then he clapped Skylar's shoulder, shook Charlotte's hand and said, "*Denki* for all you've done. I'm sorry for taking such a hostile tone."

"I understand," Skylar replied, handing him a small card. "It's my phone number and address. Keep in touch so we can update you on what we find out."

Charlotte produced a pen and slip of paper so Turner could jot down his address for them, too, but Turner hoped there would be no need to contact each other. He prayed that, when he returned home, he'd discover Jacqueline had used the spare key they'd always kept hidden by the birdfeeder and she was waiting in the parlor for Mercy and him. Barring that, he hoped he'd at least have a message from her at the phone shanty.

But there was no hint at either place to indicate his sister was still in town. And since Tessa insisted on keeping the baby with her another night, Turner's house, like his heart, felt particularly empty and stark, so he dragged himself upstairs and collapsed into bed.

Chapter Eight

For all the emotional toil Turner was suffering, Tessa was glad Mercy was none the wiser. The baby could almost manage to roll over from her back to her tummy—no small feat, considering her plumpness. She drew her knees to her belly and then kicked her legs straight, using the momentum to twist her lower body to the side, but her head and shoulders didn't follow, so eventually she'd fall to her starting position again. Tessa giggled as she watched her try repeatedly until Mercy finally became so frustrated she let out a holler, as if to accuse Tessa of not helping her.

"It's just as well you don't roll over for the first time yet," Tessa said, scooping her up. "Your *mamm* will want to be around to witness it when you do."

Mercy was drooling and pulling her ear again, sure signs her gums were bothering her. Since Tessa was accompanying Turner to the bus depot that evening, perhaps on the way they could stop to purchase a teething ring. "Meanwhile, I'll do my best to make you comfortable," she cooed to the baby.

Figuring her time caring for the baby was nearly over, Tessa wanted to make the most of every moment, and she nuzzled her cheek against Mercy's soft hair. Even after Mercy fell asleep, Tessa held her, memorizing the strawberry pucker of her mouth and the fleshy roundness of her cheeks, until her arms were nearly numb and she had to lay the baby in her makeshift crib.

It's not as if I'll never see her again. Tessa tried to assuage her loneliness so she wouldn't start weeping again. *If Jacqueline is as overwhelmed as Skylar and Charlotte indicated, she'll probably be glad to have me care for Mercy from time to time.*

She padded into the kitchen where she opened the icebox and considered preparing stew for supper. She and Turner could bring it with them in thermal mugs and eat it while they waited at the bus station. Or was that a bad idea? Did it seem like she was making a picnic of an occasion that felt more like…

well, not like a funeral exactly, but like a hospital visit? Given Turner's state of mind the previous night, Tessa wondered if he'd even be able to eat. His disappointment had been almost tangible as they'd traveled from Highland Springs to Willow Creek. She'd taken no offense when he'd hardly spoken, because she could barely form a sentence, either.

Like Turner, she'd been positive they'd catch Jacqueline at the convenience store. If Tessa felt so woefully letdown when they didn't, how must Turner have felt? No wonder he seemed pessimistic about going to the bus depot tonight—after so many stymied attempts to locate his sister, he probably had to keep his expectations in check. Admittedly, it seemed unlikely to Tessa they'd see Jacqueline there, either, but she wanted to be encouraging so she urged Turner to give it a try.

Deciding against making stew after all, Tessa peeked in on Mercy and then donned her cloak to dart down the lane to the mailbox. Valentine's Day was the following Monday and she had several cards ready to mail to her cousins in Indiana. She chortled when she removed the pile of mail that had accumulated in the box; it was a good thing her mother couldn't see how negligent she'd been in collecting it. After depositing her cards and raising the red metal flag on the side of the box, she strolled toward the house, flipping through the letters to separate hers from Turner's, since he apparently had forgotten about the mail for several days, too. Not surprisingly, most of them were hers, including one from her mother postmarked the day before.

Once inside the *daadi haus*, she put a kettle on for tea and then sat down in a square of sunlight to read her mother's letter, hoping the envelope didn't contain its usual number of recipes for her to try.

Dear Tessa,

My hand is shaking as I write this letter. This morning I crossed paths with Melinda Schrock in the mercantile.

Tessa's own hand began to tremble; she had a feeling about what was coming next.

You can imagine my shock when she expressed concern about our "family matter" that kept you from covering a shift at the shop!
While I'm sure you'll come up with an excuse for not telling your father and me

you were temporarily relieved from your duties at Schrock's, I can think of no justifiable reason why you'd lie to Melinda in order to avoid returning to work when the opportunity presented itself.

Not only is deception harmful to your relationship with God, but it undermines other people's trust in you, as well. You've long insisted you're mature enough to live on your own, but your recent behavior indicates otherwise. Your father and I have discussed the matter and we believe you'll behave more responsibly if you live with us, where we and our community can support you by holding you more accountable for your words and actions.

As a courtesy to Joseph, you may work for the next two Saturdays. By then he should be able to find someone else to fill your part-time role. We will pick you up after your shift ends on Saturday, February 19, but of course we hope for an apology before then.

Your loving (but disappointed) Mother

Tessa wanted to scream, but instead she ripped her mother's letter in half and then ripped it in half again and again and again. *How's that for immature behavior?* she railed to herself. She rose to her feet and turned the gas burner off; she was too upset to drink tea. She was too upset to do anything, except pace from the kitchen to the parlor and back again, stewing.

She should have known this was coming; after all, she had taken her chances when she turned down Melinda's shift. At the time, losing her job was a sacrifice she'd been willing to endure for Turner and Mercy. But deep down she'd doubted Joseph would feel so ruffled Tessa turned down a shift that he'd fire her. In the event she miscalculated and he did let her go, Tessa had counted on her ability to finagle another arrangement that would convince her parents she still needed to stay in Willow Creek—even if that meant being courted by Jonah. Or David. She'd never imagined the scenario she was facing now. Knowing things would turn out this way, Tessa still would have made the same decision again if it meant helping Turner find Jacqueline, but she was stunned by the reality of what the decision had cost her.

It suddenly occurred to her Melinda had gone to Highland Springs on Monday even though Tessa had refused to take her shift, which meant Joseph had been left short-handed at the shop. Tessa had automatically assumed Melinda would have forgone her trip rather than to put her employer—and her relative—in that position. Then another thought struck Tessa: What if Melinda had never actually told Joseph that Tessa had turned down the opportunity to work? What if she'd simply allowed him to think Tessa would be there? If so, when Tessa failed to show up at the shop it would have looked like Tessa was the one who didn't honor her commitment. Under those circumstances, Tessa wouldn't have been surprised if Joseph fired her before she had the opportunity to tell him she was moving back to Shady Valley.

Sitting back down at the table, she buried her head in her arms. *What does it matter if I leave Willow Creek? There's nothing for me here anyway*, she lamented. Not only was she going to lose her job, but she was about to lose Mercy, too. As for Turner, well, she never had him to lose in the first place.

I might as well resign myself to becoming Tessa Umble and making pot roasts for Melvin while he tinkers away on his buggy, she thought. But then she decided if returning to Shady Valley was the price she had to pay for helping Turner find his sister, she was going to make their efforts worth her while. She blotted her eyes with her apron, stood up and resolved to do whatever it took to reunite Mercy with her mother. And if Tessa had anything to say about it, she was also going to enjoy Turner's company while she still could.

"How was your visit with Rhoda's family?" Mark asked Patrick during their dinner break on Wednesday.

"It was enjoyable, but my stomach aches."

"You think you caught the bug?" Mark questioned.

"*Neh*, my stomach aches because every time I turned around, Rhoda's *mamm* was sliding another plate of food under my nose. I ate so much I'm surprised I could finish my sandwich just now."

Mark chuckled. "I face the same problem—Ruby's *mamm* always tempts me with food, too, which wouldn't be so bad, but Ruby is just like her. If this keeps up, I'll gain another ten pounds before summer." Mark patted his bloated stomach for emphasis.

"Some problem," Turner muttered. His brothers didn't know how blessed they were.

"What was that?" asked Mark.

"I don't think being well fed is something to complain about," Turner retorted. "You're fortunate your wives and their *mamms* are so attentive. Not everyone has someone in their lives to help provide for their physical needs as well as to encourage them emotionally and spiritually."

"I wasn't really complaining," Patrick protested. "I meant it more as a joke."

"*Jah*, well, it wasn't funny. *Kumme* on. Let's get back to work."

Turner noticed his brothers exchanging baffled looks before he walked away. He knew he was being irascible, as well as unfair. Mark and Patrick would have willingly shared the burden of Jacqueline's situation with him if Turner had told them about it. And he was just as blessed as they were—he had Tessa's help and support. But try as he did, he could neither release his anger about his circumstances nor summon any enthusiasm about going to the bus depot that evening. So, his own willpower failing him, he prayed, *Lord, please help me change my attitude. And please give me hope to keep searching for Jacqueline, just as You keep pursuing us when we turn astray. Lead her home, Lord.*

God must have answered his prayer tenfold, because by the time he arrived on Tessa's doorstep, he was humming with eagerness for their trip to the bus depot to begin.

"Hello, Turner. I didn't expect you quite this early. If you'll take Mercy to the buggy, I'll get my cloak and we can be on our way." Tessa's eyelids were puffy and her nose was pink, but she smiled at him before turning away.

When the trio was snugly situated in the buggy, Turner angled toward Tessa. If she felt ill or was upset, he wanted to give her the option of staying behind. "Are you okay?"

"Jah," she said. "Why do you ask?"

"You seem a little tired," he replied. "Or as if you've been crying."

Tessa shook her head, not looking at him. "It's nothing. I'm fine."

"You're fine now, but you were upset earlier today, weren't you?" Turner asked. In the near dark he could see Tessa's profile but he couldn't read her expression. "Don't you want to tell me what was troubling you?"

"Jah, but not now. It's a long story."

"Please?" Turner countered.

Tessa covered her face with her hands and cried. "I'm sorry. I told myself I'd keep my composure."

Knowing there was plenty of time to get to the bus depot before boarding began, Turner set the reins on his lap. Then he did something that surprised himself: he pulled Tessa's hands away from her eyes and gently turned her head so she was facing him. "No matter what it is, you can trust me," he whispered, "the way I've trusted you."

Tessa tucked her chin toward her chest and shook her head, sobbing harder. "Not yet," she uttered. "We have to find your sister."

No. For once Turner was determined to put Tessa's needs above his own need to find his sister. "Then you'd better tell me soon, because we're not leaving until you do," he said tenderly.

In tearful snippets, Tessa described her interaction with Melinda and the letter she'd received from her mother that afternoon demanding Tessa return to Shady Valley the following Saturday. When she was finished, she sat straight up again and sniffed, saying, "I'm sorry. You really didn't need to hear my problems when you've got enough burdens of your own."

"My burdens have *caused* your problems," Turner replied remorsefully, stroking his jaw. "If you weren't helping me, you wouldn't be in this predicament."

"That's not true!" Tessa declared. "If it weren't for you and Mercy, I would have had to leave Willow Creek weeks ago, because I wouldn't have been able to make my rent payment *and* buy groceries. A person can only survive for so long on pasta, you know."

Turner chuckled in spite of how guilty he felt. He'd seen enough evidence of Tessa's determination to know she would have found another way to meet her financial responsibilities if she'd had to. He was far more indebted to her than she was to him, and he was determined to help her stay in Willow Creek. Not just because he felt he owed her that much, nor because he might still need her to care for Mercy, but because he couldn't bear the thought of her leaving. "There's got to be a way we can convince your *eldre* to change their minds."

"I'm sure I'll think of something," Tessa said, although her voice lacked conviction. "For now we'd better get on the road if we want to get to the depot on time."

"All right." Turner wished there was something else he could say to buoy Tessa's mood the way she always encouraged him. But words failed him so instead he passed his handkerchief to her, picked up the reins and signaled his horse to walk on.

Inwardly, Tessa doubted there was anything she could do to stay in Willow Creek now that her *mamm*'s mind was made up. To be fair, Tessa acknowledged she hadn't been forthcoming about her situation to her parents, even if she'd withheld information for good reason. But right now she couldn't dwell on her own situation, lest she start blubbering again. As commiserating as Turner was, she didn't want to break down in front of him twice in one night. She was determined to be a help, not a hindrance, especially since she feared their trip to the depot wouldn't result in a reunion with Jacqueline, and Turner would need as much succor as she could offer.

"Ah-ah-ah," Mercy sang from her basket, snapping Tessa out of her thoughts.

"Someone's happy to be traveling," Tessa said. "Mercy loves being on the move. Have you noticed she's almost able to roll over now?"

"*Neh*, I haven't seen her try that yet. But I have noticed she's almost too big for some of her clothes."

"You're right," Tessa agreed. "*Ach!* I forgot—I meant to ask if we could stop on the way to the depot to get her a teething ring. I think her gums may be a little worse."

"Maybe on the way back," Turner suggested. "I don't think we'll have enough time now."

It felt so natural talking about mundane

errands with Turner that Tessa quickly forgot her embarrassment about crying in front of him. The closer they got to the bus depot, however, the quieter Turner became. The depot was nothing more than a square building containing a ticket booth, two bathrooms and a row of plastic seats bolted to the floor on the periphery of the room. Passengers could enter and exit the depot from a door on one end and make their way to and from the buses through the door on the other end.

"Why don't you and Mercy wait in here where it's warm and I'll go talk to the bus driver," Turner said. "I should be right back, but *kumme* find me if you spot any young women with long, dark hair. It might be *gut* to stay off to the side. I'm afraid if Jacqueline catches a glimpse of the baby, she'll know I'm here and she'll turn around and leave before I have a chance to speak to her."

Tessa nodded, even though she suspected that with her Amish attire and Mercy's babbling, which sounded especially loud in the high-ceilinged room, they were too conspicuous to be overlooked. She chose a seat affording a view out the glass door so she could watch Turner speaking to the bus driver beneath a bright overhead light. Even from a distance she could tell how tense he was by the way he massaged the back of his neck.

A few minutes later he reported the bus had just arrived from Peaksville and it was being cleaned before continuing on to Philly. No one was allowed to board until seven twenty. He said passengers could reach the bus by coming through the depot or by walking right up to it from outside. He decided to stand outdoors while Tessa and Mercy waited inside to be sure they wouldn't miss Jacqueline at either location.

Tessa watched as passengers trickled through the door. Some bought tickets at the booth; others took seats or milled about the room. She saw a businessman, an older couple and a family of five, as well as three women who appeared to be college age. When a dark-haired woman who appeared to be in her fifties and was wearing a prayer *kapp* entered the building, Tessa's heart skipped a beat. She and Turner had been so focused on finding Jacqueline, they hadn't considered what they'd say or do if they bumped into someone else from their district. Fortunately, Tessa didn't recognize the Amish passenger as being from Willow Creek. From then on, she kept her head lowered and her gaze focused on Mercy, except to furtively scan the area whenever the door opened and another person entered.

As small as the depot was, the attendant made his announcements over a loudspeaker. "Now boarding, Highland Springs to Philadelphia," he said and then repeated himself.

Tessa's heart raced. *Please, Lord, let Jacqueline show up. Please, please, please*, she pleaded silently as she wiped the drool from Mercy's chin. Tessa had put a cloth in her tote for soothing the baby's gums, but she didn't want to go wet it with cold water for fear Jacqueline would arrive while they were in the restroom.

"Now boarding, Highland Springs to Philadelphia," the attendant announced again, even though everyone except Tessa and Mercy had already filed outside. The loudspeaker crackled with static and Mercy began to whimper.

Please, Lord, I don't think Turner can take the despondency of being disappointed again, Tessa prayed. Then she got up to pace, gently joggling the baby as she circled the room. She avoided looking through the glass door—if Turner was in view, she didn't want to see the expression on his face.

"Final call for all passengers traveling from Highland Springs to Philadelphia," the man in the booth said twice and Tessa winced at the words.

A few minutes later she felt the rumble of the bus pulling away from its bay, and shortly after that a burst of cold air swept through the room when Turner opened the door. His hat was angled so Tessa couldn't see his face, but she didn't have to see it in order to know how he felt.

"Let's go," he said, his voice so low at first she wasn't sure he'd said anything at all.

Tessa stayed planted where she was. "Are you sure? Maybe she's running late. Maybe she'll show up in a minute, hoping she didn't miss the bus."

"*Neh*, she won't." Turner picked up the tote and walked to the door, holding it open for Tessa to pass through.

"I'm sorry, Turner," she said once they were on the main thoroughfare.

"Me, too."

There was nothing more either of them could say, but Mercy cried for the next ten minutes, as if to speak for them both.

"Why are we stopping here?" Tessa asked when they pulled up in front of an *Englisch* store that sold groceries, home goods and clothing.

"For the teething ring, remember? I'll calm

Mercy if you'll go in. And if you see pajamas in the next size, please get a couple of pairs of those, too. There's no sense postponing it. She's growing fast." Turner handed Tessa a couple of bills.

Tessa heard the forced nonchalance in his tone, but she understood his need to focus on practical matters and deny his despair because she had tried to do the same thing that morning after reading her mother's letter. His pain would come out sooner or later and Tessa hoped she'd be there to listen to him express it, just as he'd been there to listen to her.

"I'll be right back," she said as she disembarked the buggy.

She'd hardly taken four steps through the automatic doors when she heard someone from behind calling, "Tessa! Wait up!" It was Rhoda, Patrick's wife.

"Hello, Rhoda. How are you? Chilly evening, isn't it?" Tessa spoke rapidly, hoping to distract Rhoda from asking any questions in return.

"It's not so bad because we turned the heater on," Rhoda replied. "That's one of the really *gut* things about being married to someone who knows everything there is to know about buggies. Patrick modifies ours for as much comfort as the *Ordnung* allows. Does Turner have a heater in his buggy, too?"

"Turner?" Tessa played dumb.

"*Jah*, didn't I see you getting out of his buggy just now? Patrick will want to say hello to him before we leave."

"*Neh!*" Tessa responded sharply. "That's not a *gut* idea right now. He's…he's…" She was at a complete loss for an explanation.

"Sorry for the wait," Patrick said to Rhoda as he breezed through the doors. "Oh, hello, Tessa."

"Hello, Patrick," Tessa replied. "Don't let me keep the two of you. I think the store closes at nine."

If Tessa waited until the couple walked farther into the store, she could run back to the buggy to warn Turner. That way they could leave before Patrick and Rhoda came out to talk to him. They'd find out about Mercy soon enough, but tonight of all nights, Turner was in no shape to tell them about the baby and Tessa was going to do her best to help protect his secret for as long as she could.

"*Neh*, doesn't close until ten," Rhoda corrected Tessa. To Patrick she said, "Tessa and I are having a little chat, so you go ahead in and look for those work gloves you need. I'll meet you near the checkout counter."

Tessa sensed Rhoda wasn't going to let her question about Turner go ignored, so she confessed, "You're right, that was Turner's buggy you saw me get out of. He was so kind as to transport me here, since there's something I urgently need to buy and this is the only store that carries it."

Rhoda raised her eyebrows, leaned forward and touched Tessa's arm. "It's okay, Tessa, I won't tell anyone, not even Patrick. Your secret is safe with me."

"Tell them what?" Tessa asked, doubting there was much of anything Rhoda wouldn't tell.

"You know." Rhoda winked. "I won't tell them Turner is courting you."

"Pah!" Tessa sputtered, the air knocked out of her.

"Don't look so nervous," Rhoda giggled. "I mean it when I say I won't tell. After the last time you and I spoke at church, I had a very unpleasant experience because someone implied something about me that wasn't true. I believe the Lord used the situation to show me how harmful my own nattering could be. I'm sorry for anything I've ever repeated that I shouldn't have, and I'm committed to not sharing other people's information in the future. Even if it's something *wunderbaar*, like the news you and Turner are walking out. Trust me, you'll see. With *Gott*'s help, I'm keeping my lips sealed."

Tessa uttered the only words she could manage, "*Denki*, Rhoda," before hightailing it away from her.

Even though he had directed the horse to the farthest corner of the parking lot, Turner sat in the back of the buggy where he could cradle Mercy without being seen by any passersby. He was glad to have a few minutes to gather his wits; he'd been close to either punching something or crying back at the depot. The act of pacifying Mercy was calming to him, too.

"I know you're upset," he sympathized with the baby in a low voice. "We both are."

Upset didn't begin to cover the range of emotions he felt right then. He was also angry, grieved and downcast because they hadn't found Jacqueline—doubly so because of Tessa's news. He didn't know what else he could do to search for his sister and he hadn't any clue about how to help Tessa stay in Willow Creek, either. He felt so powerless he couldn't even muster the will to pray.

"Giddyap," he said to Mercy, bouncing her

on his knee. "This is how you ride a horse, Mercy, up and down, just like this. Giddyap."

By the time Tessa returned, the baby was squealing with delight. Turner felt a small measure of satisfaction knowing he could at least make his niece happy, even if he couldn't solve the other problems he faced.

"Quick," Tessa urged, taking Mercy from him. "We have to leave right away, before Patrick *kummes* out of the store."

Turner scrambled to take his seat again. In his haste, he momentarily forgot about his disappointment; he just wanted to flee before his brother finished shopping. When they'd put a good distance between themselves and the store, Turner eased up on his horse.

"That was close," Tessa said. "Here's your change. And an oversize heart-shaped cookie cutter."

"An oversize heart-shaped cookie cutter? Why would you buy me such a thing?"

In his peripheral vision, Turner saw Tessa dabbing drool from Mercy's chin with a cloth. "I crossed paths with Rhoda. She saw me getting out of your buggy, so I told her you brought me here to help me find a special item. Which you did, right?"

"Technically, I suppose I did. But what has that got to do with the cookie cutter?"

"I couldn't very well purchase a teething ring and baby pajamas with Rhoda and Patrick in the store because they might have seen me. But they also might have seen me leave without buying a specialty item. So, I purchased the first thing I saw that I knew the mercantile doesn't carry. I'll pay for it and keep it myself if you don't want it."

"Don't be *silly*," Turner chuckled. "Of course I want it. What man doesn't want a heart-shaped cookie cutter?"

Tessa laughed, too. "Mind you, it's not just *any* heart-shaped cookie cutter—it's an *oversize* heart-shaped cookie cutter!"

"I'm sure this will *kumme* in very handy when I host my annual Valentine's Day party," Turner joked.

"Your annual Valentine's Day party? Why haven't I ever been invited to that?" Tessa crossed her arms as if she was pretending to feel slighted.

"Because this is the first year I'm having it," Turner replied without missing a beat. Then it was as if all of the tension he'd held pent up inside him came rushing out in the form of laughter. He cracked up so long and hard he thought he might need to bring the horse to a halt.

"Don't tell me—Mercy and I will be your only guests," Tessa jibed.

"*Neh*, just you. Unless Mercy's tooth cuts through by Monday, she won't be able to eat the oversize heart-shaped cookies I plan to bake."

Tessa giggled and wiped the corner of her eye with her free hand. "There's something else I have to confess about my discussion with Rhoda. I hope it doesn't offend you."

Turner was curious. "What's that?"

"First off, let me assure you she absolutely promised not to tell anyone and I think she'll honor her word."

Now Turner was worried. "She couldn't have found out about Jac—"

"*Neh, neh*, she doesn't know anything about Jacqueline," Tessa said. "But because I told her you'd given me a ride to the store, she made the assumption you were courting me."

"That's all?" Turner asked. "Why would that offend me?"

"Because I didn't deny it. I allowed her to think you wanted to keep our courtship a secret, otherwise she would have brought Patrick over to the buggy to greet you."

"While I'm sorry my circumstances put you in that position, I understand. But as long as you're not upset about Rhoda making that assumption, then neither am I."

"I'm not upset," Tessa confirmed, repositioning Mercy on her lap.

Why? Because it isn't true so it doesn't matter what Rhoda thinks, or because you'd accept me as a suitor? Turner wondered. Merely discussing a courtship between them caused warmth to course through every fiber of his body. Turner was too flustered to say anything else until they'd almost arrived home.

"In spite of not finding my sister tonight, it felt so *gut* to laugh. *Denki*, Tessa, for helping me through such a difficult time." Turner wanted to say more, so much more, but what words could express the depth of his feelings?

"I'm not gone yet and we haven't found Jacqueline yet, so I'm not done helping you," she reminded him. "I intend to accompany you to the depot Friday evening, too."

"I'm glad," he said, but the knot in his throat at the mention of her leaving Willow Creek was so large his sentiment was barely audible.

As he brought the buggy to a stop in front of Tessa's place, she offered to keep Mercy overnight again. But Turner knew what a blow it had been for Tessa to receive her mother's letter that morning and he figured she needed a good night's rest. When he said as much, she didn't argue. So the baby wouldn't get too cold, he dropped Mercy and Tessa off at the *daadi haus* while he stabled the horse.

When he walked into the parlor, Tessa had just finished changing Mercy's diaper. He looked down at the baby, who was batting her arms and kicking her legs as if trying to get their attention.

"You're a happy *maedel*, aren't you? Is that because your *mamm* is coming home soon?" Tessa asked and Turner was heartened by her positivity. Tessa grinned a wide grin at Mercy and ran her fingers up her tummy, repeating, "*Jah*, you're a happy *maedel*, aren't you?"

Just then Mercy made a giggling noise. Turner and Tessa both looked at each other, raising their eyebrows. "Did she just laugh?" he asked.

Right on cue, Mercy undeniably gave them the sweetest laugh he'd ever heard.

"She did! She laughed!" Tessa said and she and Turner spontaneously threw their arms around each other.

Turner wished the moment—and the embrace—would never end. Right then he wanted to kiss her more than he ever wanted anything—even more than he wanted to find Jacqueline. Yet the very thought of his sister reminded him why he couldn't entertain any more notions of romance, so he dropped his arms and in a single motion lifted Mercy from where she lay.

"Say bye-bye to Tessa," he instructed Mercy, but he felt as if he could have been speaking to himself.

Chapter Nine

Tessa squirmed beneath her quilt, trying to find a position that would facilitate sleep. So much had happened that day she didn't know how to make sense of it all.

Instead of focusing on the upsetting events she couldn't control and problems she couldn't solve, she tried to reflect only on the good parts of the day. Such as the moment when Mercy laughed, and especially the moment after that, when she and Turner embraced. As if those two occurrences weren't splendid enough, there was a third happening in the sequence—the moment when Turner's face was so close to hers, and his eyes were filled with such yearning, Tessa had been certain he was about to kiss her. The mere thought of his lips on hers made her catch her breath;

if he had actually kissed her, she probably would have fainted from bliss.

Of course, he hadn't actually kissed her. They hadn't actually found Jacqueline. And she was nowhere near coming up with a reason strong enough to convince her parents she ought to stay in Willow Creek.

As her thoughts looped back to the dilemmas she and Turner were facing, Tessa allowed herself to consider the possibility it might be a long time before he found his sister; worse, he might never locate her. Either way, Turner eventually would have to tell his family and the community about the baby. Rhoda or Ruby might care for Mercy on occasion, but who was better suited to be her full-time nanny than Tessa? She didn't have to divide her attentions between other familial responsibilities like they did. Surely her parents would allow her to remain in Willow Creek to care for a baby who was essentially orphaned, wouldn't they? Just as she drifted into sleep, Tessa envisioned another possibility: Turner would ask to marry her and the two of them would raise Mercy together as their own...

But in the bright sunlight of a new day, Tessa realized how preposterous her wish was. When Turner knocked on her door, his forehead was ridged with worry lines and Tessa suspected romance was the last thing on his mind, much less marriage.

"Is it okay if I'm a little late collecting Mercy tonight?" he asked.

"Absolutely. I'd also be happy to keep her overnight again if that would be more helpful."

"*Denki*, but that's not necessary. I only need you to watch her so I can stop by the convenience store. I want to give Artie a note for Jacqueline in case she shows up there for some reason."

While Tessa was glad Turner was demonstrating renewed determination to find his sister, she was dubious about his plan. Since Charlotte and Skylar indicated Jacqueline was wrestling with other types of shame, Tessa imagined the girl would also be too embarrassed to return to the store after being fired. Besides, Artie said payday was one day and one day only. So what reason would Jacqueline have to go back there? But Tessa supposed anything was possible; besides, Turner needed as much encouragement as he could get, so she held her tongue.

Turner seemed to know what she was thinking. "Don't worry about me getting my hopes up," he said. "I don't believe she's going to visit the store, either, but I'll feel better if I do something instead of just waiting until it's time to go to the bus depot again."

"Why would you assume I'm worried? I'm *glad* you're keeping your hopes up!" Tessa protested.

This time it was a smile that caused Turner's forehead to wrinkle. "You didn't say you were worried, but you were thinking it," he bantered. "I'm getting better at reading your expressions, Tessa."

With Turner gazing at her like that with his big, soulful eyes, Tessa completely lost her train of thought and she couldn't come up with a witty response.

Fortunately, Mercy butted in. "Ah-ah-ah-ah."

"*Jah*, we see you. We know you like to be the center of conversation," Tessa said with a laugh and Mercy squawked in response. Glancing back up at Turner, Tessa asked, "Would you like to eat supper here tonight? I have all the makings for stew. I can let it simmer, so it won't matter what time you arrive."

Turner accepted her invitation, and then cupped Mercy's fat cheeks in one hand and kissed the top of her head good-bye. After he left, Tessa carried the baby into the parlor, where she pointed out the window at the tree branches swaying in the wind and the sun dappling the frozen ground with shadows. Tessa neglected her housework to hold, play with and sing to Mercy for the rest of the morning.

"There will always be floors to sweep and windows to wash," she told the baby, "but you and I won't always be togeth—" She couldn't bring herself to finish the sentence aloud. If Turner could keep his hopes up about his situation, she could keep her hopes up about hers.

Later, when she'd put Mercy down for her afternoon nap, Tessa chopped vegetables and cut the meat for the stew. She was cleaning up when she suddenly remembered Katie was supposed to visit her the following night for supper and it was Tessa's turn to cook. *But I told Turner I'd go with him to the bus depot*, she fretted. She'd have to go tell Katie tonight she needed to cancel. Since it probably would be late when Turner returned, perhaps he'd offer to give her a ride to Katie's house after supper. Tessa smiled at the thought; traveling side-by-side with Turner beneath the moonlight was so romantic, no matter their destination. But what excuse would she give her sister for canceling? Then she remembered Katie had an appointment with the doctor on Wednesday afternoon; surely she was eager to talk to her sister privately about the outcome. Tessa didn't want to hurt Katie's feelings, nor did she want to let Turner down. What was she going to do?

After brooding about it through the rest of her household chores, Tessa realized she'd have to tell Turner about the predicament. Meanwhile, there was nothing she could do now except to pray, and once she did, she felt so reinvigorated she decided to bake a pan of lemon squares. This might be one of his last opportunities to taste them. Maybe he'd be so pleased she took the time to make her specialty dessert for him, he wouldn't be able to resist kissing her.

"Ach!" she said aloud. "I'm becoming more like my *mamm* every day!"

"Rhoda called on us early this morning to say Patrick has the stomach bug and he won't be here today," Mark said after removing his hat and hanging up his coat. "I guess it wasn't his mother-in-law's cooking making his belly ache yesterday after all."

"Jah. He was well enough to be out and about last night, so that means the worst of it probably hit him during the early morning hours," Turner said, distracted by the paper-

work mounting on the desk in the corner of the shop.

"What were you two doing out and about last night?" Mark asked.

Turner jerked his head up. What did Mark mean, "you two?" Had he seen Tessa and Turner on the road? Aloud he asked, "What?"

"You just said Patrick was out and about last night. Where did the two of you go?"

Turner exhaled. "Nowhere. Not together, anyway. I crossed paths with him at the *Englisch* store in Highland Springs."

Dodging questions, hiding Mercy and trying to outpace Jacqueline's movements was wearing Turner out. He wondered if it was time to tell his brothers about the situation. Not only for his sake, but because they probably didn't know what to make of his ups and downs and he owed them an explanation for his recent moodiness. But, illogical as it was, he felt if he didn't tell them, it would mean he hadn't given up hope—hope that Jacqueline would return and hope that Tessa would be able to stay in Willow Creek. For a fleeting moment he again allowed himself to think of courting her...

"Did you hear me?" Patrick questioned loudly.

"Sorry. What did you say?"

"I asked if you want me to make the wheel delivery tomorrow morning."

"*Neh*, I'll do it," Turner replied. "And unless any new repairs *kumme* in this afternoon, let's get this order finished and then you can call it a day. I'll stay here and catch up on the accounting."

"Really?"

"Don't look so surprised," Turner chuckled. "I haven't been that demanding lately, have I? *Neh*, don't answer that. Just leave early and take your wife out to supper. You deserve a break and Ruby does, too."

Mark left at three thirty and Turner took advantage of the hushed environment to tackle the paperwork he'd put off. His progress was slow, however, and he barely made a dent in it before it was time to head to the convenience store. Tearing a piece of paper from a pad, he wrote:

Dear Jacqueline,

If you are planning to leave the area, I'd urge you to reconsider. You didn't have a choice about losing your parents, but you do have a choice about your daughter losing her mother. Mercy needs you. God forgives you. And Patrick, Mark and I love you. We'll work things out together.

Please come back to us.

Your brother,
Turner

He folded the sheet thrice and slid it into an envelope, which he sealed. Then he hitched the horse to the buggy and journeyed to Highland Springs, arriving in the lot at the same time Artie was parking his car.

The stocky man held his hands up. "She didn't come in for her pay, so I haven't seen her," he stated gruffly before Turner had a chance to greet him.

"I know. I'm here to ask if you'll give her this if she does stop by." Turner extended the envelope.

Artie shook his head but accepted the letter. "You're not going to give up, are you?" he asked.

"*Neh*. Not yet," Turner answered. *Although sometimes I sure feel like it.*

Artie galumphed into the store and Turner returned to his buggy. Although he hadn't performed much physical labor in the shop that day, Turner was tuckered out. At least he had Tessa's and Mercy's smiles to anticipate seeing at the end of his trip. But when he sat down to share Tessa's savory stew with her, her eyes appeared lusterless and she was quieter than usual.

"Patrick was out sick today," Turner said conversationally toward the end of their meal. "He came down with the stomach flu. I'm relieved you and Mercy haven't caught it."

"I guess that's one *gut* thing about being so isolated—we're not exposed to as many germs," Tessa replied as she rose to take their plates to the sink.

So, was that what was wrong? Was she tiring of being alone in the house with the baby all day?

"Is something on your mind?" he finally asked, holding Mercy while Tessa brought dessert to the table. She paused in the middle of pulling back the tinfoil covering the pan.

"*Jah*, I'm afraid there is." She reminded him that earlier in the week she'd agreed to meet with Katie for supper on Friday. "She's going to arrive at five and she usually only stays for an hour or an hour and a half at most. But if she doesn't leave until six thirty, that will be cutting it pretty close for us to get to the depot in time. I think I should cancel our supper altogether, but I don't know what excuse to give her."

Thinking it would be unfair for Tessa to change the plans she'd made with her sister so he could keep plans he'd made concerning *his* sister, Turner said, "*Neh*, don't cancel your supper. As long as Katie leaves by quarter of seven, we'll have time to spare. In fact, even if we encounter a brief delay on the road after that, we'll be fine. But if your sister stays longer than expected and you can't *kumme*, Mercy and I will make the trip by ourselves."

"I don't know." Tessa was biting her lower lip. "Are you sure about this?"

"It's all settled." Turner wiped Mercy's nose with a napkin. "So stop looking so concerned. For a minute I thought you were going to tell me something awful had happened. Like that you'd burned dessert."

Tessa's countenance lifted noticeably and a mischievous twinkle lit her eyes. "*Neh*, lemon bars are the one thing I rarely burn," she said as she cut a large piece for him. "But I'm warning you—they're extra lemony, so they'll make your lips pucker."

She blushed as soon as she said the words, as if she'd just had the same thought he did—the thought that had nothing to do with lemons, but everything to do with lips.

* * *

As Mercy slept on Friday afternoon, Tessa surveyed the food in her cupboards and icebox. She wanted to make beef stroganoff, but she discovered she didn't have any noodles in the pantry—that was a switch! She figured she could serve the stroganoff over mashed potatoes instead, until she found she didn't have any potatoes, either. She realized she had little choice but to make a haystack supper, which essentially consisted of seasoning whatever meat and veggies she had on hand and serving them over a layer of crushed crackers. Then she'd top the "haystack" with salsa and cheese. Not the fanciest meal she'd ever prepared, but Katie wouldn't mind.

When she finished chopping onions, she melted a thick pat of butter in a pan and added the onions to it. As she worked, she considered whether or not she should tell Katie about the letter from their mother. On the one hand, she thought it was only fair to prepare her sister for the probability Tessa had to return home. On the other hand, if Katie confided the doctor confirmed she was with child, Tessa didn't want to dampen her sister's joyful news. Besides, there was still time to think of some way to convince her parents she needed to stay in Willow Creek, wasn't there?

Tessa sighed heavily. She wouldn't tell her sister tonight, but she knew she ought to give Joseph the courtesy of telling him tomorrow—if he didn't fire her first. For the fourth time that day, tears rolled down Tessa's cheeks. She reflexively lifted her hand to brush them away and the onion juice on her fingers stung her eyes, causing her to weep harder. She was in the bathroom washing her face when Mercy began crying in the bedroom. The baby had soaked right through her clothes and the bedding was wet, too. Tessa knew she wouldn't have time to bathe her before Turner arrived to pick her up, so she used warm water and a cloth to clean her as well as she could. Mercy was not pleased.

"Uh-oh, Mercy," she said in a singsong voice, trying to mollify her. "It looks like we're out of clean *windle*. I need to dash to the basement and get a fresh one, okay? I'll be right back, little *haws*."

But Mercy was screaming so loudly Tessa didn't want to put her down. Because the diapers were hung so high she had to stand on her tiptoes to reach them, Tessa knew she wouldn't be able to unclasp them from the rope while holding Mercy. Instead, she one-handedly fished through the tote bag she used to carry Mercy's belongings.

"Sh-sh-sh," she said, bouncing Mercy, but the baby's cries escalated. Exasperated, Tessa dumped the tote over so she could see at a glance whether it contained any diapers. Fortunately, there was one left. As Tessa finished changing Mercy, she smelled something burning and she tore into the kitchen. Nothing was aflame but the onions were blackened and smoking in the pan. Careful to angle Mercy away from the burner, Tessa turned off the gas. At that very moment, Turner knocked.

"*Kumme* in," she shouted louder than she intended as she rinsed the pan under the tap. A cloud of steam rose around her, causing her eyes to water even more.

"Here, let me help you," Turner said when he entered, lifting Mercy from her arms.

"*Denki.*" Tessa excused herself to go into the washroom, where she washed her face a second time. *I'm a wreck*, she thought as the mirror reflected her pink nostrils, blotchy cheeks and mussed hair. At that moment, she wished Katie wasn't coming over and Mercy and Turner would just leave already. She would have preferred to spend the evening taking a hot bath, eating a store-bought pizza she heated in the oven and working on her final Valentine's Day cards.

Instead, she dried her eyes and took a deep breath. When Tessa returned to the kitchen, she found Mercy cooing to Turner. *That little scamp!* she thought wryly.

"Sorry about that," she said. "One minute I was chopping onions and the next minute…" She spread her arms to indicate the chaos.

"You must be tired," Turner replied. "Even if Katie leaves in time, are you sure you want to *kumme* with me tonight? I could go alone. It might be better if you stayed here with Mercy anyway. I can see her tooth is almost breaking through. It might make her cross."

"Neh!" Tessa answered sharply. She felt guilty for thinking it, but at that moment she decided if she couldn't stay home alone, she didn't want to stay home at all: she needed to get out of the house. "We made our plans and we should stick to them. I'll meet you at your house by six forty-five at the latest—if I don't, it means Katie is still here and you and Mercy should leave without me."

Turner seemed to be scrutinizing her and he scratched the back of his head, but he didn't argue. As soon as he and Mercy left, Tessa regretted the tone she'd taken. Then she walked into the parlor and saw the contents of the tote strewn across the floor and she became irritable all over again. First because she'd made a mess and second because Turner had neglected to ask for the tote, which contained items he'd probably need for Mercy during the next couple of hours. "Do I always have to be the one to remember everything?" Tessa grumbled.

She returned Mercy's belongings to the bag and then scoured the kitchen, washroom and parlor twice to be absolutely sure her sister wouldn't find any trace of Mercy. Then she crammed the bag under Katie's bed since Katie would never have reason to look under there. As long as she was on her knees, Tessa figured she'd better pray; otherwise, she was likely to snap at Katie just as she'd snapped at Turner.

When she was done asking the Lord for grace, as well as for Jacqueline to arrive at the bus depot that night, Tessa stood up. But Katie's bed looked so inviting she thought she'd steal a fifteen-minute catnap before starting supper—rather, before starting it a second time. *A little sleep and I'll be as fresh as a daisy,* she thought as her head sunk into the pillow.

The next thing she knew, someone was pounding on the door. She sat up, dazed.

Her sister usually tapped the door twice and then walked right in. Had Turner come back for the tote bag? Tessa hoped not: she could only imagine how disheveled she appeared. Trying to pin her prayer *kapp* into place, she swung her legs over the bed and scurried toward the door. The pounding continued and then she heard footsteps scurrying from the porch; Turner probably was afraid of being caught at her house by Katie, so he didn't want to wait any longer.

"Don't go. I'm here," she announced, swinging the door open. But he'd already left. She took a step out onto the porch. "Turner!" she called, just as she glimpsed movement from the corner of her eye.

"Surprise!" a chorus of voices shouted. Suddenly several people were singing "Happy Birthday" to her.

Tessa stayed frozen where she was, one foot inside the house, one foot outside. *I must be dreaming*, she thought. *This can't really be happening.*

But sure enough, when they'd finished singing, Katie, Mason, Faith, Hunter, Anna, Fletcher and, last but not least, Jonah gathered around her, laughing at what Tessa knew was the stunned expression on her face. She managed to squeak out the words, "*Denki*, everyone, but my birthday isn't until next Friday."

"We wanted to surprise you by celebrating early. And it looks like we did!" Katie was practically warbling with delight.

"Are you going to invite us in or are you just going to stand there gawking?" Mason ribbed and Tessa moved to the side to let them pass.

Once indoors, Katie directed the men into the parlor and then she, Anna and Faith bustled around the kitchen, uncovering the dishes they'd prepared and pulling plates from the cupboards. Tessa absentmindedly washed the burned onions from the pan, trying to surmise a reason they had to leave by six forty-five. She couldn't. It would be too insulting, too ungrateful. Turner was going to have to go to the depot without her, and he was going to have to bring Mercy with him. *But her gums are sore. She needs me to comfort her and Turner does, too*, Tessa thought, and a tear trickled down her cheek. She felt as if she'd abandoned them both.

"The birthday *maedel* needs to freshen up," she said. Katie followed her as she darted to her room.

While Tessa let her hair down to brush it, Katie confessed. "I… I got a letter from *Mamm* and I know you did, too."

Tessa nodded, not trusting herself to speak.

"That's why I wanted to have a party now, instead of next week. It's kind of a last-ditch attempt to help you get to know Jonah."

Tessa shook her head. "It's too late for that," she said as she gathered her hair into a bun. "I think it's time to give up."

"*Neh*, not yet. I'm going to tell *Mamm* she has to let you stay here because next fall Willow Creek will be short a teacher again. If you have a suitor *and* a job, she's sure to change her mind."

Tessa clapped her hand over her open mouth. Willow Creek would need a new teacher? That could mean only one thing: Katie would be resigning because she was with child. Tessa had been so shocked by the surprise party she completely forgot to ask about Katie's doctor appointment.

"Katie! What a blessing!" she exclaimed and encircled her sister with her arms. Tessa doubted their mother would change her mind, even if Tessa did wish to become the new teacher and Jonah wanted to walk out with her. But for Katie's sake she said, "*Denki* for the party. And, who knows, maybe your plan will work."

Katie beamed. "Great. But if you're going to capture Jonah's attention, you might want to put on another dress first. Otherwise he'll be focused on that blotch on your shoulder instead of your winning smile."

Tessa peered sideways at her shoulder, which was damp with Mercy's drool. Her arms suddenly ached with loneliness. She could have started weeping again but her eyes were already puffy enough, so instead she changed her dress and then joined the others in celebration.

Turner was getting nervous. It was six thirty. He couldn't wait any longer to hitch his horse to the buggy; maybe by the time he was finished, Tessa would be walking up the lane. He bundled Mercy and carried her to the stable in the basket, which he secured in the back of the buggy and then hitched the horse. Still no Tessa. He waited a few more minutes, figuring he could guide the horse into a swift trot if necessary. He had really hoped Tessa would be able to accompany him, but when he feared he could wait no longer, he started down the lane.

As he approached the *daadi haus,* Turner noticed lamps shining from several windows. Then he spotted Katie and Mason's buggy secured to the hitching post he and his brothers built primarily for Katie and Tessa's use back when they still had a horse. *I wonder why Katie hasn't left*, Turner mused. *Of all evenings, it had to be tonight that she chose to stay late.*

He sighed as Mercy fussed behind him. He assumed she was irritable because her gums hurt, but without Tessa's input, he couldn't be certain. He hoped once they were on the main road, the motion of the buggy would calm her. He was nearing the end of the lane when he spied a buggy hitched to the fence straight ahead, blocking his way. He brought his horse to an abrupt stop. Who would have been so rude as to block the lane and so reckless as to tie a horse to a flimsy fence railing instead of to the hitching post?

Then it dawned on him: whoever was in his way was a guest at Tessa's house. It was probably one of the Fishers' relatives or their friends from out of state joining them for supper, because anyone local would have known the lane was shared by both Turner and Tessa; it wasn't meant for Tessa's use alone. Now what was he going to do? Time was of the essence. He couldn't leave Mercy alone in the dark buggy at the end of the lane, nor could he risk Tessa's guests seeing her. Since fencing lined both sides of the narrow lane, there wasn't enough room at this particular juncture to turn the buggy around. So he directed his horse to walk backward toward the *daadi haus*.

It was a slow process, but when he arrived at a spot close enough for him to keep an eye on the buggy, he jumped out of the carriage and bound up the porch steps. He repeatedly rapped the door. A moment later, Tessa appeared.

"Turner, you're still here! What's wrong?" she asked in a surprised voice. "Is Mercy—"

"Hush!" He put his fingers to his lips. What was she thinking? Her guests could have heard her.

"Who is it, Tessa?" Katie asked over Tessa's shoulder. "Oh, *gut*, it's Turner. I haven't seen you for a long time. Please, *kumme* join our party. We were just about to serve cake. Faith Schwartz baked it, so you know it will be *appenditlich*."

"*Neh*, I can't," he gruffly declined. "There's somewhere I need to be and one of your guests is blocking the lane."

"*Ach*, that must be Jonah's buggy. I'll get him."

When Katie left the room, Tessa hurriedly whispered, "I'm so sorry I can't go with you. You see, my sis—"

Turner cut her off. "No need to explain, but

tell *Jonah*—" Turner practically spat out Jonah's name "—to hurry it up. I'll be waiting outside." Over his shoulder he added, "And in the future, I don't ever want to find a horse hitched to the fence again."

Turner wasn't angry simply because the buggy was blocking his way; he was also miffed because the fence wasn't at the correct height to tether a horse. The animal could become agitated and try to rear, snapping the wooden rail and injuring itself.

Furthermore, he was piqued Tessa was hosting a party when she'd promised to accompany him to the depot. He knew she wouldn't have deliberately misled him about her plans, so he suspected she'd made the party arrangements long ago and had since forgotten about them. Even so, she knew how important it was for him to get to the depot in time. She should have made doubly sure there were no obstacles to slow him down. Better yet, she shouldn't have invited a guest who was so irresponsible and inconsiderate he'd tie his horse to a fence railing unsuited for hitching purposes.

A very tall young man jounced past his buggy. Jonah, no doubt. Turner couldn't help but speculate about whether he was also at Tessa's the night the group played Cut The

Pie. It seemed to take him forever to reposition his horse and buggy, but once the lane was finally clear, Turner wasted no time hurrying past him and onto the main road.

Turner's horse accelerated into a swift gallop and within minutes, Mercy's whining subsided. He knew without looking at her she'd fallen asleep. Turner's jaw ached but he pleaded aloud with the Lord to deliver him to the depot on time or else to delay the bus's departure.

When they arrived, he rapidly but securely hitched his horse and lifted Mercy from her basket. She stirred but didn't wake. He clutched her to his chest with both arms to shield her from the cold and sprinted to the bus depot.

Panting, he asked the ticket booth attendant, "Has the seven-thirty-eight bus to Philadelphia left yet?"

"Yes, sir. It departed right on time. You missed it by two minutes."

Groaning, Turner shut his eyes and pinched the bridge of his nose. He felt as if the room was tilting. He couldn't fall over, not with Mercy in his arms. Steadying himself against the ledge of the ticket counter, he asked, "Did you notice if a teenage girl boarded it? She would have had long dark hair and she was probably traveling alone. She's slim and about this tall." Turner indicated the height of his shoulder.

"I see so many passengers after a while they start to look alike," the attendant said. "But, yes, there might have been someone matching that description who boarded the bus. I only remember her because she counted out her change down to her last dime in order to purchase the ticket. She must have been awfully desperate to get away from here."

Turner staggered backward as if he'd been shoved. His voice reverberated in the empty room as he repeatedly moaned, *"Neh, neh, neh!"*

Jolted awake, Mercy raised her voice, too, so Turner returned with her to the buggy, where he tucked her into the basket as she continued to holler. He wanted to holler, too. His disappointment this time was three-fold: he was disappointed in his sister, disappointed in Tessa and, dare he think it, disappointed in God. It was time to give up searching and praying he'd find Jacqueline, and it was definitely time to stop depending on Tessa or imagining any kind of romantic future with her. *I'm all done*, he thought and headed for home.

Chapter Ten

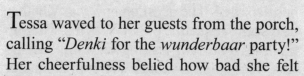

Tessa waved to her guests from the porch, calling "*Denki* for the *wunderbaar* party!" Her cheerfulness belied how bad she felt about Jonah blocking Turner's path.

But how could he have known she shared a lane with Turner? The two times Jonah visited the property it had been too dark for him to see that the lane continued past the *daadi haus* and up the hill. According to her sister, Jonah had traveled alone, and she and Mason transported Anna, Fletcher, Faith and Hunter to the party. Katie had instructed Jonah not to bring his buggy to the hitching post at the *daadi haus* until after they sang, because if Tessa spotted it their surprise would be ruined. Jonah had intended to tie his horse to the fence for only a minute, but in all of the excitement, he'd forgotten to return to it and move his buggy.

It was a perfectly understandable mistake, but Tessa didn't blame Turner for being brusque. He was probably already on tenterhooks when Tessa hadn't shown up in time to accompany him to Highland Springs. But recalling that Turner said he'd have plenty of time even if he encountered a delay, she assumed he'd reached the depot before the bus departed. The question now was whether he'd seen Jacqueline or not. Was his sister up the hill right now, visiting with him? If she was, Tessa didn't want to interrupt them, but if Turner hadn't found her, Tessa wanted to offer consolation.

I know—I'll bring Mercy's tote bag up to the house. Tessa figured if Jacqueline was there, she'd give Turner the bag and leave them to their privacy. Otherwise, she'd stay to explain about the party and the fiasco with Jonah's buggy, and help Turner devise a new course of action. She pulled the tote from beneath Katie's bed, put on her cloak and hurried up the hill.

Before she had a chance to knock on the door, she heard Turner's voice from the other end of the porch. "Don't knock. You'll wake Mercy."

"You startled me," she said, making her

way to him in the dark as a cloud passed across the moon. "Is… Is Jacqueline home?"

"Neh," he replied tersely.

"Ach, I'm sorry to hear that, Turner. And I'm sorry I couldn't accompany you. I was—"

"You were having a *wunderbaar* party, I know. I heard." In the moonlight, Turner's profile looked as if it was chiseled from stone; his jaw was hardened in an uncompromising line.

Despite Turner's accusatory tone, Tessa responded softly, *"Jah*, my sister and friends threw a surprise birthday party for me. I felt terrible I couldn't accompany you, but asking them to leave early would have been rude."

"Not half as rude as it was for them to block my way."

Tessa's eyes smarted but she understood how shattered he must have felt because Jacqueline wasn't at the depot a second time. She hesitantly explained, "Jonah didn't know we share the same lane. He moved the buggy as quickly as he could."

"It wasn't quick enough." Turner's voice was flinty with resentment when he said, "The bus departed two minutes before I arrived. Two minutes, Tessa. And according to the station attendant, Jacqueline was on it."

"Oh, *neh. Neh!*" A spasm gripped Tessa's stomach and she felt woozy. If she was this devastated, she could only imagine how Turner felt. She took a deep breath and said, "That's *baremlich*, but at least we know she went to Philadelphia. Skylar and Charlotte said they had contacts throughout—"

"Enough!" Turner yelled, facing her. "Enough is enough. I'm done looking for her, but even if I weren't, I don't want Skylar and Charlotte's help."

"Okay. We don't have to involve them. We'll find her ourselves. I still have a week here to keep helping you." Tessa touched Turner's shoulder but he jerked his arm away.

"*Helping* me?" he ridiculed. "If it weren't for *your* party, *your* guests and *your* insatiable need to have *schpass*, Jacqueline would be here right now! What kind of help is that?"

Now it was Tessa's turn to flinch. "What are you saying? You can't possibly be blaming me for *your* late arrival at the depot! You said you'd allow yourself plenty of time to get there, even if there was some kind of delay. Besides, I had no idea about the party and no idea about the buggy."

"Maybe not, but that doesn't make you any less responsible. A person is known by the company she keeps, and it's not the first time you've associated with someone who behaves in a harebrained, juvenile or otherwise feckless manner!" Turner pivoted to walk away, adding, "It's no surprise your *eldre* want you to *kumme* home where they can monitor your behavior."

Tessa darted ahead of him and planted herself in front of the door, glaring. Her words were like knives on her tongue when she snarled, "Do you want to know what's no surprise, Turner? What's no surprise is that your sister ran away and won't *kumme* home. Who would ever want to live with such a judgmental, unappreciative, boring old man?"

Then she pushed past him and stormed down the hill, slamming the door so hard the windows rattled. She marched straight to her bedroom, picked up her pillow, pushed her face against it and screamed until the back of her throat burned. She had dedicated the last three weeks to protecting Turner's secret and caring for Mercy, day or night, whenever he needed. She had risked her job so Turner could look for Jacqueline. And she had lost the privilege of living alone as a result of putting Turner's and Mercy's needs ahead of her own. How could Turner have the nerve to imply she'd rather have fun than help him find Jacqueline? How could he imply she was

immature or undependable? Tessa covered
her face with the pillow and screamed again.

Then she pulled her suitcase from the closet
and flung her dresses, capes and aprons atop
the bed. She yanked her good church prayer
kapp from the peg on the wall and emptied
her drawers of their stockings and hair pins.
She wished she didn't have to wait until next
Saturday to leave. She had half a mind to call
her parents from the shanty and ask them to
pick her up on Monday.

*Turner won't last three days without me to
help him care for Mercy*, she gloated. But at
the thought of leaving Mercy abruptly, just as
Jacqueline had done, Tessa's emotions turned
from outrage to anguish. She sat on the edge
of the bed and a torrent of tears washed down
her cheeks. She sobbed so hard she could
barely breathe and she knew she'd make herself sick if she didn't stop.

By the time she washed her face and
donned her nightclothes, Tessa was too
drained to hang up the clothes and put away
the items she'd flung on her bed, so she shuffled into Katie's old room. As she lay her
head down, she felt a soft lump beneath her
neck. She was about to turn on the lamp to
see what it was when she realized she was
holding the cloth Amish puzzle ball she'd

made for Mercy. "My little *haws*, what are you going to do without me?" she murmured. "And what am I going to do without you?" Then she cried herself to sleep.

Turner checked on Mercy and then reclined on his bed with an extra pillow folded beneath his neck to ease the pain. It wasn't helping much but he wouldn't have been able to sleep anyway. After missing the bus's departure by two minutes, Turner didn't think he could possibly experience any more dejection that evening, but Tessa's words had wounded the rawest, most vulnerable part of him. They wouldn't have hurt so much if they hadn't been true: he'd always known if only he had been a better father figure or a stronger role model of their Amish lifestyle and Christian faith, Jacqueline would have made different choices.

As insufferable as that reality was, Turner had to face the fact he couldn't do anything about the past. But he could try his best to make sure he didn't fail Mercy the way he'd failed Jacqueline, and he resolved to tell his brothers and their wives about the baby. Since Patrick was still recovering and business was slow, Turner had told Mark not to come to the shop on Saturday, which meant Turner would have to wait to talk to his brothers until he could pay them a visit after church on Sunday. Together as a family, with counsel from the deacons, they'd decide what was best for Mercy. Although Turner still felt conflicted about betraying Jacqueline's confidence, in a way it would be a relief he didn't have to hide Mercy from his brothers or the community any longer. Now maybe he'd have someone other than Tessa to count on for help.

The next afternoon while Mercy napped, Turner opened the ledger he'd brought home on Friday so he could continue trying to reconcile their accounts at home. When he finished, he took a brief snooze until Mercy's jubilant babbling woke him. To Turner's surprise, when he entered her room, she was lying on her stomach. *Wait until I tell Tessa Mercy rolled over.* The thought instantly flitted through his mind before he remembered what happened the night before.

When he picked Mercy up, he noticed her clothes were damp. "Let's change your *windle* and then you can show me your new trick," he said as he searched her dresser for a clean diaper. When he couldn't find one, he brought the baby downstairs to check the tote Tessa left on his porch the previous evening, but he didn't find one there, either.

Turner glanced at the clock: it was a little past four. Tessa wouldn't be home from Schrock's until after five and Mercy's clothes were soaked through. Even if he could wait until Tessa returned, he didn't want to speak to her if he could avoid it. He wrapped the baby snugly and lifted the spare key to the *daadi haus* from the hook near the door. Ordinarily, he wouldn't think of entering the house without Tessa's permission, but he figured under the circumstances it was permissible. Tessa wouldn't even have to know he'd been there.

Tessa trudged home from Schrock's, completely spent. On the way to work that morning she'd planned what she'd say to Joseph if he was upset about being short staffed the previous Tuesday, as well as how she was going to tell him she was resigning, in the event he didn't fire her first. But when she arrived at the shop it was Amity, not her husband, who greeted Tessa in the back room. She said Joseph and the children had come down with the stomach bug, as had Melinda and Jesse, and she asked if Tessa could possibly manage the store on her own.

"The shop only needs to stay open until the three-o'clock-tour-bus customers leave.

You know how important their sales are to our success," Amity had explained.

"Of course," Tessa had agreed. She owed Joseph that much. Besides, waiting on customers would keep her mind off her own queasy stomach, a nausea that wasn't caused by the flu.

"*Denki.* Joseph said he knew he could count on you." Amity had confided, "He wasn't pleased when Melinda asked you to take her shift on such short notice, and he was even less pleased when she went to Shady Valley even though you couldn't cover for her."

While Tessa was relieved to discover Joseph knew it wasn't her fault he was left on his own in the shop on Tuesday, she'd been abashed at Amity's praise. Joseph's gratitude was going to make it that much harder for her to tell him she was leaving Willow Creek. She'd agonized over it most of the day, and by the time the final customers left she had a headache as well as a stomachache.

She was slogging up the lane to the *daadi haus* when a female voice called, "Excuse me, please."

Standing beneath the big willow tree near the porch was an *Englischer*.

"*Jah?*" Tessa replied warily. The last thing

she needed was for Turner to see another *Englischer* on his property. Who knew what conclusions he might jump to about "the company she kept."

"I'm looking for Turner King. I checked at the house but he's not there. Do you know if he's in town?" As the girl approached, Tessa caught sight of her eyes. She knew those eyes: they were Turner's eyes. Mercy's eyes. Tessa felt her heart fluttering within her ribs.

"He was here as of last night. He's probably running an errand," she replied, although she couldn't imagine him going out with Mercy. "Why don't you *kumme* inside with me to get warm while you wait for him."

Jacqueline nodded and followed Tessa indoors. Tessa offered the girl a chair by the wood stove in the parlor and then she put on a kettle for tea. As she waited for it to boil, she prayed that God would guide her conversation with Turner's sister. Tessa didn't know whether she should reveal that she knew who Jacqueline was or not. As angry as she was at Turner, Tessa had given him her word she wouldn't tell anyone she knew about Mercy, and Tessa figured that meant not telling Jacqueline, either.

"Sorry, the cookies aren't from scratch," Tessa said nervously a few minutes later as she carried the tray into the room. The men had gobbled up all of the homemade goodies the night before, so there weren't any leftovers.

"*Denki.* I like this kind," Jacqueline replied. Her hand trembled so much her teacup rattled in its saucer. Tessa was quiet, allowing her to lead the conversation. "How long have you lived here?"

"About two years. My sister lived here with me until she got married last November."

Jacqueline set her cup on the end table. "Then I believe you must know about my *dochder*, Mercy?"

Tessa's cheeks burned as she nodded.

"It's okay. From what my friends told me, I realize they'd taken Mercy to the wrong house. I don't care about any of that. I just want to know if she's all right."

Tessa nodded again before finding her voice. "She's thriving."

"Are you sure? You've seen her again since that night?"

"I... I've been helping care for her. Your *dochder* is just the sweetest baby. She laughed at us the other day for the first time. She can almost roll over and she's cutting a tooth. I'm Tessa Fisher, by the way," Tessa jabbered.

"I'm Jacqueline," the girl said, even though

Tessa already knew her name. "*Denki* for looking after my Mercy while I was…while I was away. I'm glad Turner had your help."

"It was my pleasure. And rest assured no one else knows about you or the baby."

Jacqueline hung her head. "Turner must be so ashamed—I certainly am. I wouldn't blame him if he's really angry to see me traipsing back here again after leaving Mercy with him all that time."

"Angry to see you? Are you kidding me? Turner can't wait to see you!" Tessa knew she was raising her voice but she couldn't help herself. She had to impress upon Jacqueline how keenly Turner wanted to welcome her home. "I don't think you have any idea how deeply he's grieved your absence and worried about your well-being! I don't think you understand how steadfastly he's searched for you!"

Jacqueline's eyes were tearful and her chin quivered, so Tessa rose, crossed the room and leaned down, placing her hands on the girl's shoulders. "Turner didn't tell anyone about the baby because of *your* request. He was also trying to shield you from gossip. Believe me, there were plenty of times when it would have been easier for everyone if he had disclosed your secret. But he didn't because he's so loyal and protective and loving. Angry? *Neh.* He's going to be *thrilled* to see you. There's nothing he's wanted more than to *wilkom* you home."

Jacqueline wiped her cheeks with the back of her hand. "I'm glad, because I've *kumme* back for *gut.*"

"You have? That's *wunderbaar!*" Tessa spontaneously embraced the girl as if Jacqueline was her own sister and Jacqueline hugged her back. After they let go, Tessa started to say, "Why don't we—" but she was interrupted by a faint noise coming from the basement.

She jerked the door open to discover Turner standing at the bottom of the staircase with Mercy in his arms.

Shocked, Tessa yelped, "What in the world?"

"Ah-ah-ah," the baby chanted.

From the parlor, Jacqueline squealed, "Is that Mercy? My Mercy?"

Turner rushed up the stairs and squeezed past Tessa to get to his sister, who sobbed upon seeing her child.

"Mercy, my *bobbel,*" she kept repeating, taking the baby from Turner and kissing her all over her cheeks and head. "Look how you've grown!"

Meanwhile, Turner cried, "Oh, Jacqueline, how I've prayed for your return." He embraced both mother and child, closing his eyes as he hugged them. Tessa noticed a tear dribble down his face and she glanced away, feeling as if she was intruding on their reunion.

When he finally let go of Jacqueline and Mercy, Turner said, "Mercy needed clean *windle*, so I let myself in. Then I heard voices coming from upstairs and I didn't know who it was. Since I didn't want anyone to find out about Mercy, I just stayed where I was, hoping they'd leave. I didn't mean to startle anyone."

His tone was more informational than apologetic and Turner neither looked at Tessa nor addressed her by name, so she responded by simply murmuring, "Hmm," without looking at him, either.

He quickly said, "*Kumme*, Jacqueline, let's go to the house."

"Okay," she agreed. Her face was tear streaked. "Tessa probably doesn't want us blubbering in her parlor all evening. I'll change Mercy's clothes and *windle* at your house."

Turner glanced around the room. "Do you have a suitcase?"

"*Jah*, I left it on your porch."

At the door Jacqueline swiveled to face Tessa. "I can't express my gratitude enough, Tessa. Mercy is going to miss you. But you can *kumme* up the hill to visit us every day, can't she, Turner?"

"*Neh*, she can't," he said sharply. Opening the door, he explained, "She's moving next week."

But Tessa knew the real reason he didn't want her to visit. He shouldn't have worried; she had no intention of darkening his doorstep again until she returned the key to the *daadi haus*.

Bit by bit over the next several hours, Jacqueline told Turner about the *Englisch* boy she'd met during *rumspringa*. Once they learned she was with child, the boy dumped her. Jacqueline was so humiliated and ashamed she left Louisa's and secured a job as a live-in nanny for an *Englisch* Christian family in Ohio, who knew of her plight and provided her with medical care as well as room and board and nominal wages. Although they encouraged her to return home, Jacqueline was convinced once the baby was born, the boy would want to marry her. Instead, he denied knowing her and his parents threatened to call the police if she continued "stalking" him.

Disgraced and deserted, Jacqueline boarded a bus to Willow Creek, but on the way she lost her nerve and made it only as far as Highland Springs. She spent most of her savings to sublet a dingy room in a rundown house. After the landlady somehow found out Jacqueline was from an Amish family, she took to disparaging her faith.

Around that time—because she needed to save every cent she could for formula—Jacqueline began attending the free suppers Skylar and Charlotte hosted at their home. They encouraged her to stay in the area and think things over, even if she wasn't ready to return to her family. That's when she left the baby with Turner—or rather, Skylar and Charlotte did. Meanwhile, Jacqueline took a job at the store where Skylar worked. By then she was so ashamed and downtrodden, she figured Mercy would be better off without her, and she decided she'd board a bus and move to Philadelphia on her own. Right around the time she made up her mind to leave, she got fired.

"I'm so glad you didn't have enough money to pay for a ticket," Turner said, sighing heavily.

"Oh, I had enough money—*just* enough.

And I mean down to the penny," Jacqueline replied. "In fact, I even bought the ticket. I was going to leave on the seven-thirty-eight bus last night."

Turner suppressed a gasp. "Then what stopped you?"

"I love Mercy too much," she said, gazing at the baby as she rocked her. "I'm so sorry for what I did. I know it was wrong. But that doesn't mean I regret giving birth to Mercy. It doesn't mean I don't love her with my whole heart."

"I know."

"Turner, I am so sorry for what I put you through, too. Will you forgive me?"

"*Jah*, I forgive you. Will you forgive me for…for failing you?"

Jacqueline's eyes flashed as if he'd said something insulting. "Failing me? How have you ever failed me?"

"I—I didn't know how to raise, how to guide you once you became a teenager. I probably made a lot of mistakes when you were younger, too. I'm to blame for—"

"For *nothing*!" Jacqueline stopped rocking the chair and leaned forward. "Turner, my running away had absolutely nothing to do with you. It had nothing to do with Ant Louisa. I was being headstrong. I was following my own will instead of *Gott*'s will for me!"

Turner was surprised by Jacqueline's perspective; she demonstrated so much more accountability than he'd expected.

"Why do you think I left Mercy with you?" Without waiting for an answer, Jacqueline spouted, "Because I knew you'd be as *gut* of a parent to her as you have been to me."

Overwhelmed, Turner's eyes filled. After all this time of blaming himself for somehow failing Jacqueline, and after all this time of thinking he never ought to marry, he could hardly believe his ears when Jacqueline called him a good parent.

She continued, "And because of my upbringing, I realize it's time for me to grow up and admit my wrongdoings. So I've confessed them to the Lord and I'm prepared to speak to the deacons. I want to be baptized into the church, Turner. I want to raise Mercy the way you and Louisa raised me."

Denki, Lord, Turner prayed, wiping his sleeve across his eyes.

Jacqueline fawned over Mercy, "I can't get over how much you've grown. And look at that smile! Your *onkel* took *gut* care of you, didn't he?"

"I couldn't have done it without Tessa's

help," he replied. Despite their argument the previous night, Turner had to give credit where credit was due.

"Hey, I know! Monday is Valentine's Day. Let's invite Tessa over for a special supper. We'll ask Skylar and Charlotte to *kumme*, too."

Turner hedged. "Uh, I don't know if that's a *gut* idea…"

"Why not? I'll take care of all the arrangements, I promise. Besides, don't you think we should do something nice for them, as a way of expressing our gratitude?"

Put like that, Turner couldn't say no, but he cautioned, "I don't know if Tessa will *kumme*. She probably has packing to do."

"She'll *kumme*. She's crazy about Mercy, and from the way she talks about you I would have thought you were courting her."

Turner coughed. "What? Why do you say that?"

"Well, for one thing, when I was nervous about how you'd feel about seeing me again, Tessa reminded me of how loving, protective and loyal you are. But it wasn't just what she said. It was also the way her face looked when she said it. You could tell she really meant it."

As Turner recalled their argument on Friday night, a searing pang of compunction rendered him speechless. At the same moment, the baby curled her fingers around Jacqueline's hair, which hung loose in an *Englisch* style.

"You'd better get used to that," Turner said. "She was always pulling Tessa's *kapp* strings and she's bound to pull yours, too."

"I don't mind at all. But I do mind that *schtinke*—I'd better change her *windle*. After I put her down, I think I'll turn in for the night."

Turner retired to his room, too, where he sat on his bed and mulled over his sister's remarks. Did Tessa really mean it when she'd said he was loving, loyal and protective? That wasn't how he had acted toward her on Friday night. That wasn't how she'd described him on Friday night, either. *Of course, she may have been speaking in anger, reacting to the vicious, unfounded comments I'd made about her*, Turner reluctantly admitted to himself.

It's time for me to grow up and admit my wrongdoings, Jacqueline had said. How was it possible his seventeen-year-old sister was behaving more responsibly than he was? Turner dropped to his knees and spent the better part of the next hour confessing his transgressions and thanking God for bringing Jacqueline safely home. Before climbing into bed, Turner asked the Lord to ease the hurt he'd caused Tessa to suffer and to soften her heart toward him so they could be reconciled.

The next morning he traveled alone since his sister and the baby wouldn't be attending church until Jacqueline spoke to the deacon and bishop. He was glad to see Patrick sitting a few benches in front of him; Turner assumed he was no longer contagious, which meant he could carry out the plan to visit his brothers later that afternoon. After eating dinner and helping the other men stack and carry the benches to the bench wagon, Turner tried to track down Tessa, but by then she must have either left with Katie and Mason or walked home through the fields. He'd have to wait until evening to speak with her.

Turner stopped at his house only long enough for Jacqueline to climb into the buggy with Mercy. As they rolled down the lane toward the road, he sighted Tessa walking in their direction.

"Stop," Jacqueline demanded. "I want to tell Tessa about the party."

So Turner brought the buggy to a halt and held the baby while Jacqueline hopped down to speak with Tessa. He could hear their conversation clearly.

"*Guder nammidaag*, Tessa," his sister chirped.

"I'm so glad I caught you, because I want to invite you to our Valentine's Day party tomorrow night at six o'clock."

Turner saw the look of utter disbelief on Tessa's face. He wondered if he should step down and say something to encourage her to attend. But what would he say?

Jacqueline must have noticed her expression, too, because she pleaded, "Please *kumme*. After all you've done for me, the least I can do is have you as my special guest for supper."

"*Denki*, that's very kind, but I have chores to take care of before I leave."

Jacqueline wasn't giving up. "But Mercy has been asking where you are. She really wants to see you."

Turner chuckled: his sister was hitting Tessa's soft spot.

At that, Tessa conceded, "All right, but I won't be able to stay long."

"See?" Jacqueline said when she was seated beside Turner again. "I told you she'd *kumme*."

When they arrived at Mark's house, he and Patrick were astounded to see Jacqueline and they couldn't stop hugging her. Amazingly, neither Ruby nor Rhoda asked any questions—they were too busy oohing and aah-

ing over Mercy. Before their visit was over,
Jacqueline had invited all of them to the Valentine's Day party, too.

By the time they returned home, it was
nearly nine o'clock and there were no lamps
shining at the *daadi haus*. Disappointed,
Turner slipped out onto the porch after Jacqueline and Mercy went to bed. He rubbed
his jaw—why was it hurting so badly? He
shouldn't be tense; he should be overjoyed.
Jacqueline was home, safe and sound, which
was the only thing he wanted. Or was it?
Peering down at the darkened *daadi haus*, he
had to acknowledge there was something else
he desired: he desired to walk out with Tessa.
But how could he? He didn't even know if
she'd forgive him, much less accept him as a
suitor. Not to mention, she was leaving Willow Creek in less than seven days.

Suddenly, Turner recalled Artie asking,
You're not going to give up, are you? And
he was emboldened by the memory of his
own response, *Neh. Not yet.* Right then and
there he decided he wasn't going to give up
on his dream of courting Tessa. *Not yet,* he
thought. *Not ever.*

But the next evening, as he waited for Tessa
to arrive at the party, he felt his resolve giving way to nervousness. He didn't suppose

he'd get a chance to talk to her in private until after the party, but he intended to try to put her at ease in his presence until then.

His brothers and their wives showed up first, followed by Skylar and Charlotte.

"I'm so glad you're here!" Jacqueline squealed when she saw them.

"*We're* so glad *you're* here," Charlotte answered.

Jacqueline ushered them into the parlor to meet the rest of the family, while Turner lingered in the kitchen until Tessa knocked on the door.

He grinned and said, "Happy Valentine's Day, Tessa."

"Hello, Turner," she replied, neither warmly nor coolly. "There's a car parked in the lane, but it's got nothing to do with me."

Remembering how harshly he'd spoken to her about Jonah, Turner felt his ears burning. "*Jah*, in daylight you'd recognize it belongs to Charlotte and Skylar. They're in the parlor."

"You've invited *Englischers* into your home?"

"Why not? As a very wise young woman once told me, they just have a different way of living out their faith than we do." Turner's remark elicited a quick smile from Tessa and his confidence surged.

During supper everyone complimented Jacqueline on the meat loaf, brown-butter mashed potatoes and broccoli bake she'd prepared, but by that time Turner had grown nervous again and he could hardly taste the food. For dessert the group devoured yellow cupcakes with red-and-pink buttercream frosting Rhoda purchased from Faith Schwartz's bakery, as well as strawberries dipped in chocolate Ruby brought. Afterward, the women shooed the men into the parlor. Turner tried to focus on their conversation to no avail, so he was glad when he realized the stove would need more wood soon and he went outside to fetch it.

By the time he'd returned, the women were sitting in the parlor, too, and Jacqueline was handing out slips of paper for a game of charades. Hoping he could be on Tessa's team, Turner set the wood in the bin. "Where's Tessa?" he asked, looking around.

"She just left. She said she had to call it an early night."

Turner didn't bother to excuse himself. He bolted out of the house, hurtled down the porch stairs and zoomed down the hill, reaching Tessa just as she was shutting the door behind her.

Breathless, he choked out the words, "Tessa, please wait. I need to talk to you."

She gave him a curious look but opened the door for him to pass through. They went into the parlor and she took a seat on the sofa. He knelt in front of her but she looked down at her hands instead of into his eyes. This time he hadn't rehearsed what he was going to say; he wanted it to come straight from his heart.

"Tessa, I am so sorry for the *baremlich* things I said Friday night. I didn't mean a word of them. I was so disappointed because I thought I'd missed Jacqueline and I needed to blame someone. So I blamed the Lord and I blamed you—the very ones who faithfully helped me all along. But the truth was, *I* was the one to blame. I didn't leave enough time to get to the depot because I kept hoping if I waited long enough, you'd be able to accompany me."

Tessa bit her lip and nodded. The delicate tip of her nose was turning pink and it seemed she might begin to weep, but instead she said haltingly, "I understand. And I... I forgive you, Turner." When she finally lifted her head, her expression was fraught with candor. "I'm sorry I called you judgmental, unappreciative and boring. You're not any of those things. I never once heard you condemn your sister the way most people in your situation would. You've always expressed your appreciation of me, in both word and deed. And I've never had such interesting conversations with a man as I've had with you."

A smile crept across Turner's face, but he still had more to say. "You've helped me so much these past few weeks, Tessa. Now it's my turn to help you. If you'll allow me, I'd like to speak to your parents."

"And say what?"

"Say what I should have said as soon as I found out about the letter you received from your *mamm*. I'll tell them about Jacqueline and Mercy. I'll say you're the most thoughtful, capable, mature woman I've ever met. Not only that, but your sense of *schpass* has lifted my mood when I've needed it most. I'll remind them they asked me to keep an eye out for you, but instead you kept an eye out for me." Turner paused to catch his breath. "I'll tell them how much I want you to stay here."

Tessa's eyes glistened. It felt like months had passed since the last time Turner beheld her face. "But why?" she asked. "Jacqueline is home now. You don't need my help anymore."

He swallowed, gathering courage. "I want you to stay because I want to court you, Tessa."

She blinked. She blinked again. A smile flickered across her lips, slowly at first, but then spread like wildfire from her mouth to her cheeks to her eyes, until all of her features were illuminated by its brilliance. "I want to be courted by you, Turner."

He kissed her then. And then again. When he pulled away he gently traced her exquisite nose with his fingertip.

"Do you know something?" he asked. "Your *mamm* is wrong."

Tessa knitted her eyebrows. "Wrong about what?"

"The way to a man's heart isn't through his stomach. At least, that's not the way to my heart."

Tessa giggled. "*Neh?* Then what is the way to your heart?"

"The way to my heart—" he murmured, pausing to kiss her a third time "—is through *your* heart."

This time, Tessa kissed *him*. "Happy Valentine's Day, Turner," she said.

Epilogue

"These cookies are enormous!" Jacqueline exclaimed to Tessa. "Where did you get such a big cookie cutter?"

"It was Turner's, if you can believe it," Tessa answered, winking at her husband before she bit into a heart-shaped confection.

"It's a *gut* thing Mercy's asleep, or she'd be asking for a bite," Jacqueline said, looking at Mercy, who had fallen asleep on her lap. She finished the last of her cookie and then slowly stood up, careful not to rouse her daughter. "*Denki* for supper, Tessa. It was yum-yum, as Mercy would say. I'd better head down the hill now."

"I'll walk with you back to the *daadi haus*," Turner offered.

Last year, after he and Tessa explained the situation with Mercy and Jacqueline to Tessa's parents, and in light of the fact Joseph restored Tessa's full-time schedule as well as gave her a promotion, Waneta and Henry agreed to allow their daughter to continue living in the *daadi haus*. When Turner and Tessa married in the fall, Jacqueline moved into the *daadi haus* and Tessa moved up the hill.

"Could you please retrieve the mail, too?" Tessa requested. She hadn't forgotten to collect it; she'd deliberately left it in the box for Turner to find.

She was rinsing the last pot when he passed through the kitchen with a stack of wood in his arms. A few minutes later he returned from the parlor, rested his chin on her shoulder and hugged her around the waist from behind.

"I love you," he whispered into her ear.

Tessa wiped her hands on her apron and turned to face him. Wrapping her arms around his neck, she said, "I love you, too." Eager to have him read the card from her, she barely paused before asking, "Did we get any mail?"

"One for you, one for me. I must be becoming more social—this is the first time I've ever received as much mail as you," Turner joked, holding a pink envelope above Tessa's head. "A kiss for the mail carrier first."

"Silly," she said, standing on her tiptoes to kiss him and grab the letter at the same time. "This one looks like it's from my *mamm*. Please let me read it before you open yours."

They moved to the parlor where Tessa sat beneath a lamp and Turner wiggled close to her on the sofa. The card had a picture of a cupcake on the outside. Printed inside was the message Hope Your Valentine's Day Is Extra Sweet. Tessa smiled at the irony: the card was store-bought instead of handmade.

On the back Tessa's mother had written a note, which Tessa silently read to herself:

Dear Tessa,

I trust this letter finds you and Turner well. Please give him warm regards from your father and me.

As you know, Katie, Mason and little Michael are here for a visit. Your brothers' children enjoy entertaining their newest cousin with silly faces and chasing him as he crawls around the house. It reminds me of how your brothers and sister used to dote on you when you were a baby.

To a mother, her children will always

be her babies in some way, no matter how old they are. (You'll understand when you have one of your own.) We all wish you and Turner were here with us. We look forward to visiting you next.

Your loving Mother

PS The enclosed recipe for boneless pork roast with vegetables is from Bertha Umble. I think ten cloves of garlic is too much, so I only use half that many and it turns out fine.

Tessa dabbed her cheek; she was touched by her mother's sentiments. Even the recipe card made her lonely.

"Are you okay?" Turner gave her a squeeze.

"*Jah*, just a little homesick. Can you imagine—I'm homesick for Shady Valley?"

"We can go there whenever you want."

"*Jah*, it would be fun to surprise my *mamm* and *daed*," Tessa said. "Now it's your turn. Open your card."

Turner let go of her so he could open his mail and Tessa watched his expression as he pulled the card from its envelope. On the front, she'd used red and white construction paper to form two interlocking hearts. On the inside were three of the same type of hearts. Beneath them she'd written a rhyme:

> Husbands are sweet.
> Babies are, too.
> I'll soon be blessed
> And so will you!

Turner's mouth fell open as the meaning of the verse sunk in. "R-really?" he asked.

"Really," she confirmed.

"Oh, Tessa, my Tessa!" he shouted.

He hugged her so tight she giggled and said, "I can't breathe."

Turner immediately loosened his grip. He slid one hand behind her head and tenderly caressed her cheek with his thumb as he looked into her eyes.

"I wonder whether *Gott* will bless us with a girl or a boy. Either way, I'll be happy. But I do hope our *kin* inherits your profile," he said. Then he added, "Your *mamm* and Katie will be thrilled. So will Jacqueline. But poor Joseph—wait till he finds he's going to lose his assistant manager!"

Tessa giggled. "Well, we don't want to tell anyone about the *bobbel* just yet. Let's wait a while, okay?"

"Of course," Turner said. He rubbed his nose against hers and then gave her a kiss. "It will be our little secret."

* * * * *

*If you liked this story,
pick up these previous books in Carrie
Lighte's Amish Country Courtships series:*

Amish Triplets for Christmas
Anna's Forgotten Fiancé
An Amish Holiday Wedding

Available now from Love Inspired!

*Find more great reads at
www.LoveInspired.com.*

Dear Reader,

I confess Tessa and I share the same perspective about cooking: If I'm the only one eating, why go through the trouble of preparing a full meal? When I was much younger and single, my cupboards were just as bare as Tessa's were, too. I'll never forget the time my parents came to visit and my mother marveled at how spotlessly clean my oven was. Little did she know that was because I hardly ever used it. (Actually, she probably did know; mothers are clever like that.)

Also like Tessa, I make *appenditlich* lemon squares, if I do say so myself. I'd give you my recipe, but it's a closely guarded secret—although it's not nearly as big as the secret Tessa and Turner shared.

Thank you for reading their story. There are two more books to come in the Amish Country Courtships miniseries and I hope you'll enjoy them.

Blessings,
Carrie Lighte

Get 4 FREE REWARDS!

We'll send you 2 FREE Books plus 2 FREE Mystery Gifts.

Love Inspired® Suspense books feature Christian characters facing challenges to their faith... and lives.

FREE
Value Over
$20

YES! Please send me 2 FREE Love Inspired® Suspense novels and my 2 FREE mystery gifts (gifts are worth about $10 retail). After receiving them, if I don't wish to receive any more books, I can return the shipping statement marked "cancel." If I don't cancel, I will receive 4 brand-new novels every month and be billed just $5.24 each for the regular-print edition or $5.74 each for the larger-print edition in the U.S., or $5.74 each for the regular-print edition or $6.24 each for the larger-print edition in Canada. That's a savings of at least 13% off the cover price. It's quite a bargain! Shipping and handling is just 50¢ per book in the U.S. and 75¢ per book in Canada.* I understand that accepting the 2 free books and gifts places me under no obligation to buy anything. I can always return a shipment and cancel at any time. The free books and gifts are mine to keep no matter what I decide.

Choose one: ☐ **Love Inspired® Suspense**   ☐ **Love Inspired® Suspense**
                   Regular-Print   **Larger-Print**
                   (153/353 IDN GMY5)   (107/307 IDN GMY5)

Name (please print)

Address   Apt. #

City   State/Province   Zip/Postal Code

Mail to the Reader Service:
IN U.S.A.: P.O. Box 1341, Buffalo, NY 14240-8531
IN CANADA: P.O. Box 603, Fort Erie, Ontario L2A 5X3

Want to try 2 free books from another series! Call 1-800-873-8635 or visit www.ReaderService.com.

LIS19R

Get 4 FREE REWARDS!

We'll send you 2 FREE Books plus 2 FREE Mystery Gifts.

Harlequin® Heartwarming™ Larger-Print books feature traditional values of home, family, community and—most of all—love.

FREE
Value Over
$20

YES! Please send me 2 FREE Harlequin® Heartwarming™ Larger-Print novels and my 2 FREE mystery gifts (gifts worth about $10 retail). After receiving them, if I don't wish to receive any more books, I can return the shipping statement marked "cancel." If I don't cancel, I will receive 4 brand-new larger-print novels every month and be billed just $5.49 per book in the U.S. or $6.24 per book in Canada. That's a savings of at least 19% off the cover price. It's quite a bargain! Shipping and handling is just 50¢ per book in the U.S. and 75¢ per book in Canada.* I understand that accepting the 2 free books and gifts places me under no obligation to buy anything. I can always return a shipment and cancel at any time. The free books and gifts are mine to keep no matter what I decide.

161/361 IDN GMY3

Name (please print)

Address   Apt. #

City   State/Province   Zip/Postal Code

Mail to the **Reader Service:**
IN U.S.A.: P.O. Box 1341, Buffalo, NY 14240-8531
IN CANADA: P.O. Box 603, Fort Erie, Ontario L2A 5X3

Want to try 2 free books from another series! Call 1-800-873-8635 or visit www.ReaderService.com.

2018 LOVE INSPIRED CHRISTMAS COLLECTION!

You'll get 1 FREE BOOK and 2 FREE GIFTS in your first shipment!

This collection is guaranteed to provide you with many hours of cozy reading pleasure with uplifting romances that celebrate the joy of love at Christmas.

YES! Please send me the first shipment of the 2018 Love Inspired Christmas Collection consisting of a FREE LARGER PRINT BOOK and 3 more books on free home preview. If I decide to keep the books, I'll pay just $20.25 U.S./$22.50 CAN. plus $1.99 shipping and handling. If I don't cancel, I will receive 3 more shipments, each about a month apart, consisting of 4 books, all for the same low subscribers-only discount price plus shipping and handling. Plus, I'll receive a FREE cozy pair of Holiday Socks (approx. retail value of $5.99)! As an added bonus, each shipment contains a FREE whimsical Holiday Candleholder (approx. retail value of $4.99)!

☐ 286 HCN 4330   ☐ 486 HCN 4330

Name (please print)

Address   Apt. #

City   State/Province   Zip/Postal Code

Mail to the **Reader Service:**
IN U.S.A.: P.O. Box 1867, Buffalo, NY. 14240-1867
IN CANADA: P.O. Box 609, Fort Erie, Ontario L2A 5X3